STAR WARS
LAST OF THE JEDI

STAR WARS

LAST OF THE JEDI

AGAINST THE EMPIRE
BY JUDE WATSON

SCHOLASTIC INC.

New York   Toronto   London   Auckland   Sydney   Mexico City   New Delhi   Hong Kong   Buenos Aires

ISBN-13: 978-0-439-68141-4
ISBN-10: 0-439-68141-3

Cover art by Drew Struzan

12 11 10 9 8 7 6 5 4 3 2 1   7 8 9 0 1 2/0

Printed in the U.S.A.   40
First printing, October 2007

GUIDE TO
CHARACTERS

THE LAST OF THE JEDI

Obi-Wan Kenobi: The great Jedi Master, now on exile on Tatooine

Ferus Olin: Former Jedi Padawan, once apprenticed to Jedi Master Siri Tachi, currently a double agent against the Empire, on the planet Bellassa.

Solace: Formerly the Jedi Knight Fy-Tor Ana; became a bounty hunter after the Empire was established

Garen Muln: Weakened by long months of hiding after Order 66; resides on the secret asteroid base that Ferus Olin has established

Ry-Gaul: On the run since Order 66; found by Solace

THE ERASED

A loose confederation of those who have been marked for death by the Empire who gave up their official identities and disappeared; centered on Coruscant

Dexter (Dex) Jettster: Former owner of Dex's Diner; has established a safe house in Coruscant's Orange District

Oryon: Former head of a prominent Bothan spy network during the Clone Wars; divides his time between the secret asteroid base and Dex's hideout

Keets Freely: Former award-winning investigative journalist; now hiding out in Dex's safe house

Curran Caladian: Former Senatorial aide from Svivreni; cousin to deceased Senatorial aide and friend of Obi-Wan Kenobi, Tyro Caladian; marked for death due to his outspoken resistance to the establishment of the Empire; lives in Dex's safe house

GUIDE TO
CHARACTERS

KEEPERS OF THE BASE

Raina Quill: Renowned pilot from the planet Acherin's struggle against the Empire

Toma: Former general and commander of the resistance force on Acherin

THE ELEVEN

Resistance movement on the planet Bellassa; the group is beginning to be known throughout the Empire; first established by eleven men and women but has grown to include hundreds in the city of Ussa with more supporters planetwide

Roan Lands: One of the original Eleven; friend and partner to Ferus Olin; killed by Darth Vader

Dona Telamark: A supporter of the Eleven; hid Ferus Olin in her mountain retreat after his escape from an Imperial prison

Wil: One of the original Eleven and now its lead coordinator

Dr. Amie Antin: Loaned her medical services to the group, then joined later; now the second-in-command

GUIDE TO
CHARACTERS

Trever Flume: Ferus Olin's thirteen-year-old companion, a former street kid and black market operator on Bellassa; now an honorary member of the Bellassa Eleven and a resistance fighter, undercover at the Imperial Naval Academy on Coruscant.

Clive Flax: Former musician and corporate spy turned double agent during the Clone Wars; friend to Ferus and Roan; escaped with Ferus from the Imperial prison world of Dontamo

Astri Oddo: Formerly Astri Oddo Divinian; divorced the politician Bog Divinian after he joined with Sano Sauro and the Confederacy of Independent Systems during the Clone Wars; now on the run, hiding from Bog; expert slicer specializing in macroframe computer code systems

Lune Oddo Divinian: Force-adept eight-year-old son of Astri and Bog Divinian

Linna Naltree: Medical expert who helped Trever escape

Flame: Mysterious and wealthy friend to the Eleven and other resistance groups

CHAPTER ONE

His short life had been marked by megatons of bad luck, but at least Trever counted himself lucky in one respect: Regular attendance at the Ussan Day Academy was no longer required.

When his father and brother were killed by Imperial forces after the Clone Wars, his world had imploded. Everything had stopped making sense, and going to school had made the least sense of all. So he had closed the door to his old life and left it forever. He'd become a street kid, a thief, a con. Then he'd found out that Ferus Olin, the guy who let him sleep in his back room, used to be a Jedi, and the next thing he knew . . . *wha-woosh*, he was running blockades and dodging stormtroopers.

Top of the list of things he never expected to do again: go to school. So much for *that* idea. He was now a fresh recruit at the Imperial Naval Academy on Coruscant. Why couldn't he have gone undercover someplace *fun*, like a space station cantina in the Outer Rim?

Because Lune Oddo Divinian, the Force-sensitive son of Astri Oddo, had been kidnapped by his father and sent here. And Astri was frantic to get him back. So Trever had offered to enroll, make contact, and get both of them out in a couple days' time.

At least that was the plan.

To Trever, school had always felt like jail. But the Imperial Naval Academy *really* felt like jail. There were no stun cuffs or energy cages, but there was a state-of-the-art security system, ID badges, and old B-1 series battle droids from the Clone Wars that had been reactivated and reprogrammed for security. They were still in temporary quarters that the Empire had requisitioned, an old hospital built of gray synthstone. The place had no windows and still smelled of bacta.

He looked like every single one of these other recruits, with freshly-trimmed hair cut close to his skull, tunic and pants the color of a swamp, and the stupidest little cap he'd ever had the misfortune to have plopped on his head. Trever slipped it off and crammed it into his pocket. He had left behind his clothes and possessions at the check-in, and now he had to find his quarters.

The halls were empty at the moment. It was class time. All of the recruits were sweating over holo-books, and soon he'd be joining them for some new-moon fun.

"Hey, gravel-maggot!" the sharp voice called from behind him.

Trever kept walking. He wasn't here to become involved in student disputes.

"I'm talking to you, gravel-maggot!"

Unless, of course, some idiot bully tried to get in his face.

Trever turned. A tall recruit with three silver bars on his chest stared him down.

Keep your cool, Keets Freely had instructed him. Keets had researched an article on the Imperial Academy when it was still in the planning stages. Back when Keets was a journalist, before he'd managed to get a death-mark on his head after he'd angered the Empire several times. *You're a new recruit. You're the bottom of the heap. Just about everyone is allowed to torture you. It's part of the process. They want to turn you into an Imperial. They want to break you down and build you up again. Whatever you do, don't lose your temper.*

"Where's your cap, gravel-maggot?"

Oh. The cap. Trever reached into his pocket and took it out.

"You're required to wear it at all times."

"Nobody told me. Sorry. I just got here a couple of minutes ago," Trever said.

"Put it on now, gravel-maggot!" The tall recruit slapped it out of his hand and it fell on the floor.

"Now that was counterproductive," Trever said.

An interesting thing happened when this particular recruit got upset. His cheeks went pale but his neck flushed. If Trever had been on the streets of Ussa, he'd comment on it. Call the guy a ruby-throated kete and take off. Trever was a better runner than a fighter.

What bullies didn't understand was that you had to *particularize* your insults. Anybody could call anybody a gravel-maggot, for moon's sake.

But he wasn't supposed to lose his cool. He was Lune's best hope of getting out of here.

"Pick. It. Up." The other student spit out each word.

Trever picked it up. He put the cap on his head.

"Uniform delinquency and insubordination." The recruit's lip curled. He moved closer. "Bad luck on your first day. You're dead." And suddenly there was a blaster barrel pointed at Trever's chest.

The guy wasn't just a bully, he was a lunatic! Trever's knees almost buckled. After all this, after all he'd been through, this couldn't happen. Not here.

He felt an unpleasant sting.

"Ten degrades," the student said, and strode away.

What just happened? Trever wondered. What was a degrade? Sweat trickled down his back. He thought he'd stared death in the face.

Shaken, he made his way to his quarters. He had his own small room, just enough for a sleep couch and a small dresser.

They isolate you first, Keets had explained. *Part of*

*the breakdown of your personality. They don't want you
to have personality, kid.*

Shelves flipped up and down for work spaces. Trever
stowed his gear and bounced on the sleep couch. Not
very comfortable. The small pillow was like a rock.

He had noticed a supply closet on the way in. Trever
slipped out and went down the hall, alert for other students and that fake blaster. He pushed open the supply
closet door.

Ah. Stacks of blankets and pillows. He quickly
snatched a few pillows and went back to his room. He
tossed them on his bed. Might as well be comfortable
while he was here.

"Activate message unit." The voice was insistent
and came from a control panel near the door. A red light
was blinking. Trever pressed his thumb onto a sensor
panel to identify himself.

*"Recruit Fortin, report to Lieutenant Maggis,
Guardian Advisor, for orientation interview,"* the
voice said.

Fortin was the name on the false ID docs Dex Jettster
had gotten for him. Dex and Keets were both members
of the Erased, who had obliterated their former identities in order to hide from the Empire. Dex had set up a
safe house in Thugger's Alley in the Orange District,
a place buried so deep in the Coruscant underworld that
even the Empire didn't want to go there. They'd drilled
him back at the safe house, calling him by the name

over and over, going over his story until he thought he'd dive out the window.

Trever left his quarters and headed for the turbolift. He had been given the lieutenant's office number when he arrived, and he knew it was close to the office where he'd first checked in. He'd taken a placement exam just that morning, and the results had been tabulated. He hoped he wouldn't get thrown out on his ear. Academics had never been his strong suit.

He made his way to the office and activated the signal light that would tell Lieutenant Maggis that he was waiting.

Trever pulled at the collar of his tunic. He wasn't used to wearing such tight clothing. He'd be blowing this joint as soon as he could figure out a way to smuggle out Lune.

It hadn't been hard to enroll him. Not with the devious experts around him. For the first time in his life, he had a spotless academic record. Keets Freely had added the extra touch of fabricating some articles he'd supposedly written for his school paper, all about how the galaxy was a place of justice and order since the Empire took over. Pure swill, of course, but when you looked up his fake ID through the usual channels, that's what you found.

He hoped it all would hold up under Imperial scrutiny. He wasn't the smartest life-form in the quad. If he flunked the placement test, he'd be kicked out on his first day.

The door hissed open.

"Come in, already!" an impatient voice barked.

Trever had been expecting a standard Imperial officer. They all seemed to be in the mold of the Emperor — or, at least, the way Palpatine used to look before he turned into a horror holo. Tall, gray, pale. Bloodless.

But this officer was short, with a barrel chest and a big thatch of black unruly hair. His chubby cheeks gave him a boyish look, but his scowl was adult-nasty. His officer's cap was sitting askew on a glowlamp, as if he'd tossed it across the room when he'd taken it off.

Maggis had his head close to the datascreen. "Fortin. Abysmal on academics . . . mathematics, atrocious. Science, miserable. Historical comprehension, beneath my contempt." Maggis looked up at him with pure disgust. "In short, you are the sorriest recruit I've seen yet. How did you get accepted?"

Trever tried to look smarter. "I guess I was nervous when I took the placement test."

"But. You tested high on reflexes and piloting. We're looking for pilots. So welcome to the Imperial Navy. If you don't flunk out."

"Thank you."

"Thank you, *sir*."

"You're welcome."

"I'm not thanking you, you idiot. Always use 'sir' when speaking to a superior officer. That would be me."

"Yes, sir."

Maggis looked at the datascreen again. "The other encouraging news is that in barely an hour here, you've managed to rack up ten degrades. Fortin, you are aware, aren't you, that fifty gets you kicked out?"

"They didn't tell me that, sir. They didn't even tell me what a degrade *was*."

"We don't tell you everything. You're expected to find things out for yourself." Maggis leaned back and smiled. "And if you're thinking that getting kicked out isn't such a bad thing, let me explain. You don't get to leave. You get to go to the Mining Corps and serve out your time there. So if I were you, I'd follow the rules."

"But what if I break a rule while I'm trying to find out what the rules are?"

Maggis's smile grew broader. "I guess you're out of luck."

Trever swallowed. He hadn't signed up for this crazy talk. Not at all.

"We do recognize, however, that you might need some help from time to time. We assign you an older recruit who will serve as your mentor while you're here. I see you've already met him."

Trever had a sinking feeling.

"Recruit Kestrel. Apparently you had a problem

with your cap. Well. I'm sure he'll be helpful to you despite the fact that he shot you this morning. And then one day, if you're very, very good, you'll get to have a fake blaster and scare new recruits yourself." Maggis clicked a few keys. "You're due in advanced piloting in two minutes. Lateness gets you docked another degrade."

"Can you direct me to the class, sir? I wasn't given a printout of the building."

"Do I look like a traffic control droid?"

Great. Just great. Trever turned to go.

"And Fortin?"

"Sir?"

"You've got another five degrades on your record. I'd put back those pillows, if I were you."

CHAPTER TWO

Ferus Olin was having trouble with his concentration. He was losing track of things, forgetting what he was supposed to be doing while he was doing it. His surroundings no longer seemed vivid. Voices seemed to come at him from far away. Sometimes someone would speak for minutes at a time, and though he thought he'd been listening, he would have no idea what had been said.

It was not a good situation for a double agent.

Was this what grief was like? This wasn't sadness like he'd felt before, when a friend or someone he'd known well had died. It wasn't how he'd felt when he'd learned the fate of all the Jedi. That had been a blow he'd felt keenly, as though he'd been split open.

This was worse.

He'd stood by and watched, too slow to react, as Darth Vader had casually flipped his lightsaber and ran it through his best friend, his partner, Roan Lands. He had watched Roan die. Had held onto him, locked eyes with him, and said a private good-bye.

He didn't think he had ever hated anyone this much before. It wasn't part of what he was. Being trained by Jedi bred detachment into his bones. But as he had learned to love in a personal, particular way, so had he learned to hate. Learned in one instant when Vader struck.

It was amazing that he was still alive. He had attacked Vader, and Vader had handled him with ease, left him hanging in the air helplessly, even laughed at him. He had been thrown in a cell and was waiting to die when the Emperor had visited him. Ferus didn't know why the Emperor had offered him a way out. Maybe he wanted to play with Vader, irritate him by pardoning Ferus. Maybe he had bigger plans. Ferus didn't care. He'd been allowed to walk out of a prison cell. Right now that was enough. He'd deal with the rest later.

Emperor Palpatine had offered him training in the dark side of the Force, and he had accepted. Because he knew there was only one way to eliminate his pain. One way to get his revenge. Take what the Emperor offered, learn how his power worked, and then use it against Vader.

If he'd still been a Jedi, if he'd been able to talk to Mace Windu or Yoda or Obi-Wan Kenobi about the offer of a Sith Lord, they all would have said the same thing: *Do not listen. Walk away. He will corrupt you.*

11

But that was the old way. That was the way of the Jedi who were gone now. All powerless. Because they didn't believe the Sith had anything to teach them.

What if that wasn't true? What if a Jedi could learn from a Sith, gain power and multiply his gifts, but remain a Jedi?

When he'd been alone in that cell, his cheek against the floor, Ferus had not wanted to live. The only thing that had raised him up from the floor was Palpatine's offer. The only thing that gave him life was the possibility of revenge.

The Emperor had also offered him a job he couldn't refuse. He was now in charge of the effort to find Force-sensitive beings or Jedi who had escaped Order 66. The Emperor had dismissed ex-Senator Sauro from the task, saying it took one Force-sensitive to find another. Ferus would soon have access to the list.

He had already created a secret base on a constantly traveling asteroid that was surrounded by a dense atmospheric storm. His friends Raina and Toma were building shelters, setting up defense and comm systems. So far he'd only brought them Garen Muln, but soon — as soon as he was sure he'd helped all the Jedi he could — he would retire there with the ones who wanted to come. They would wait there until it was time to strike back at the Sith.

So he had a place to bring them. If he could find them. So far he hadn't had the best of luck.

He hadn't been able to discover more than hints here and there. Hints of a large-scale operation with no name. And a snare operation called *Twilight* that he suspected was targeting . . . a planet? An organization? Something big. He had to keep going, had to find out what the Emperor was planning, if he could.

He walked through the hallway of the Imperial garrison on Bellassa. Thanks to the Emperor's promise, he no longer had to travel with stormtrooper escorts. Darth Vader had been reassigned to a different garrison, one the Empire was building in the mountain area that had been giving them so much trouble. There was no danger of running into him here. Ferus didn't want to run into him.

Not until he was ready.

Ferus accessed the door panel to the training room. It was empty, as it often was at this hour. He had just had a holographic meeting with the Emperor that morning. He had been given his first lesson.

It's easier than you think, Palpatine had said. *Oh, later there will be techniques to study, exercises to complete. But to start, you must do what you were taught never to do as a Jedi. Feel your anger, but do not let it go. Feed it. Anger wants to grow. As Jedi, you fought anger's nature. It is why you lost. So this is your first lesson, Ferus. Give in to your anger. Don't let it go.*

Palpatine had smiled. *No lightsaber necessary.*

Ferus walked to the middle of the room, his boots striking the hard permacrete. In order to do this, he would have to revive his worst memory. The one he tried to bury.

In his mind, the image flicked on.

The lightsaber. The point of impact. Roan's face when the lightsaber made contact.

The jolt of the impact, the way Roan's arms went out, the way his body folded in half.

Darth Vader standing, not looking at Roan, not caring. Looking at Ferus. Killing Roan just to get at him. Eliminating a person with blood and bone and memory and laughter and vision and love, just . . . to rile a rival. As a game. As a sport.

The anger was a roar inside him. He didn't turn away. He felt it move and he brought back the same image again, brought it back so that it was imprinted on the back of his eyeballs, until he screamed out loud with his pain.

Something ripped from the wall and rocketed across the space. A brace that held up an exercise bar. Ferus opened his eyes and concentrated his gaze on that bar, heavy durasteel two meters thick. It, too, ripped from the wall and flew across the space. It smashed into the wall, and a sizeable chunk of it fell away. He felt a flood of satisfaction move through him.

He turned. A chair resting against a wall shot forward. Another. He held the objects in the air. Then he focused his anger like a laser and felt it build and build until the objects smashed together and fell, broken, to the floor.

He wasn't finished yet. Not with his anger, not with this room. This room, these objects, could be smashed and broken, and if anyone cared and came after him, they would be smashed, too, because his anger was that huge.

The floor under his feet began to crack. A chunk of ceiling fell and wires spilled out, and still Ferus kept turning, his eyes burning and the anger now a rolling ball of flame inside him until he couldn't see anything but red. Red was the color of destruction.

"What's going on here?"

The Imperial officer stood in the doorway, his eyes wide.

Ferus came back to himself. He looked around. The room was destroyed.

He had never been able to do such a thing before. He was panting. The dark side of the Force had entered him, and the pleasure he'd felt was frightening. Frightening . . . and satisfying.

Giving the officer a look of contempt, he walked out the door. The officer scurried backward in fear. Ferus enjoyed his fear.

It was the first time since Roan's death he did not feel pain.

CHAPTER THREE

Flame paced back and forth in the front room of the safe house. Time was running out on this mission. She had the resistance leaders of significant Core and Mid-Rim planet systems in her movement. The Outer Rim was too unsettled, too insignificant to worry about yet. What she really needed was for Bellassa to join Moonstrike. Even if the resistance here had become fractured, it could rise again in a heartbeat. And the symbolic weight of the Bellassan Eleven was huge. That would keep the others close.

Bellassa first. Then Coruscant. Moonstrike would be complete. Her job would be done. She would have linked the resistance movements of the most important planetary systems in the galaxy. No one thought it could be done, and she had done it.

She had come a long way from Acherin. She had thought only a few years ago that the Clone Wars wouldn't touch her. She'd thought that her comfortable life would last. She hadn't been able to imagine her world destroyed, her wealth in danger, her family dead. She had to remake herself. She had to become a warrior. She had to use all her cunning, all her will, to do it. She had succeeded. Now the one important thing in her life, the only important thing, was her mission.

If these people here didn't mess up the whole thing.

The sticking point was Bellassa. Since the death of Roan Lands and the arrest of Amie Antin, Wil had grown silent. Trever had smuggled out information that the Empire was building a toxic weapons delivery system on Ussa, and the info had been sent out to the city. It had been highlighted on the underground holo-print news, and the news had spread from citizen to citizen. Ussans had been outraged and there had been sporadic protests. Two days ago they had all stayed in their homes, refusing to work, and the city had shut down. The streets and air lanes had been eerily empty.

It had been a lesson for Flame. It was amazing what resistance could do.

The Imperial governor had retaliated by rounding up the children of the Bluestone Lake district and bringing them into the garrison jail. He threatened to send them off-planet to an Imperial prison, then move on to the next district, and the next, until the citizens went to work again.

Every Ussan had gone back to work the next day.

The children had been released, but now every Ussan

knew to what lengths the Empire would go. The Empire had set up more checkpoints on the streets. If an Ussan was caught without ID docs, he or she was immediately taken to the garrison prison.

Flame paused in her pacing, hearing the murmur of voices. She couldn't make out the words. Something was brewing, but she didn't know what, because Wil wasn't talking. Dona had arrived, and they had been in that room for over an hour now.

When would the Eleven let her into their confidence? They had allowed her to stay in the safe house, but discussions were held behind thick security doors, with her on the other side. This was the main problem in making Moonstrike work — trust. Of course, she understood that the members of any resistance group would be wary. They had to be. She had overcome that distrust before by funding the movements or taking the same risks, becoming involved in their covert operations. Group after group had come to trust her. But the Eleven was harder to crack.

Flame saw the alarm light go on, which meant someone was approaching the safe house. She went to the one-way window and looked out. She knew that Wil would be doing the same in the other room. It was Ferus Olin, walking down the ramp toward the front entrance.

Flame studied him for a moment. Unlike Wil, who was paler than ever since Amie had been captured, Ferus didn't show his grief on the outside. He looked the same. Yet she'd heard from Dona how destroyed he'd been by Roan's death.

She wasn't sure. Ferus was supposed to be a double agent, working for the Empire but keeping his ties to the resistance. Yet he appeared to be in the Emperor's good graces. She didn't know why the resistance leaders trusted him the way they did. No one was incorruptible.

Wil emerged from the inner room to open the door for Ferus. He walked in and nodded at Flame before placing a hand on Wil's shoulder. The two men looked at each other for a moment.

"I have news of Amie," Ferus said.

Wil went gray.

Ferus squeezed his shoulder. "No, she's alive. She's being transferred."

Wil swayed for a moment, relief on his drawn features. "Come inside. We'll talk. Dona is here."

"No," Flame said. "Wait."

They turned, impatient to be gone. But she wouldn't let this moment pass. It had to be now.

"I'm wasting my time here," she said. "I need Bellassa for Moonstrike. But if you don't trust me, I can't stay. There are other planets, other systems I need to contact."

She saw the hesitancy on Ferus and Wil's faces. She wasn't sure if she should push it. She had to be careful.

She didn't want to lose Bellassa. She wasn't willing to lose it. But they had to think she was.

"I can help you. You know I can. You know that without me your resistance will wither and die. Now is the moment to make your decision. Because if not, I'm gone. I don't have any more time to give you."

She watched their faces carefully. She saw doubt on Wil's, but Ferus was better at concealing his feelings. It was Ferus who had the most to lose, she knew. She could turn him in to the Empire at any time. Ferus was the one she had to win over. They didn't trust each other, but they had to find common ground, or Moonstrike would fall apart.

"Don't go," he said. "Let Wil and me talk for a moment. Then we'll call you in."

She knew then that they would accept her. They just didn't know it yet.

She inclined her head. Relief flooded her, but she didn't let them see it.

As soon as the door hissed shut behind them, Wil turned to Ferus. "How is Amie?" he asked.

"She hasn't been tortured," Ferus said. "But I've learned they're transferring her off-planet to a prison world."

Dona rose from her seat by the window. Her broad, lined face was full of worry. "We can't let that happen."

"No," Ferus agreed, "we can't. She won't survive there."

"What about Flame?" Wil asked. "Should we involve her?"

"She's right. She's wasting her time if we don't let her inside the Eleven. And what she's offering can help us. Especially now."

"What do you mean?"

"If we're to have any effective resistance on Bellassa, we have to make sure the children are safe."

"Evacuation?" Dona asked.

"Possibly. It might come to that. We couldn't pull off that sort of massive operation without help."

"Do you think we should include her, then?"

"I think we should give her a test. We'll involve her in the operation to rescue Amie, but she won't know the details. That way, Amie will be safe, but we'll have the benefit of Flame's expertise. She's an incredible pilot."

"Tell us your plan," Wil said.

"I don't have a plan, exactly. Just some ideas. I've got the transfer point and the time — we have two days."

Wil frowned. "That's not much time to plan. I don't want to endanger Amie. Maybe we should attack from the air."

"They'll be expecting that. They won't be expecting a rescue effort here. The crackdown has shut down the city. They won't imagine we'll be able to pull it off."

Dona placed her broad hands on her knees. "Then we do it here."

"How?" Wil asked. "Where is the transfer point?"

"They're using the Imperial landing platform outside the hangar on the outskirts of the city. That hangar is restricted to high-priority traffic. We'll have to rescue her, then take her through Ussa to here. I don't think we can risk taking her off-planet."

"Take her all the way through the city? That's insane," Wil said. "Do you know how many checkpoints we'd have to get through?"

"I know exactly how many. We can use some of the safe passages the Eleven have worked on."

"But they aren't complete!"

"There's a tunnel under the lake."

"It's not complete, either."

"Well, we'll have to work on it, then," Ferus said. "It's going to have to be ready in two days. In the meantime, we get the strike force together."

Wil nodded, thinking hard. "It will take time. My best operatives are in the mountains now."

"Don't worry," Ferus said. "I have a strike force on the way."

CHAPTER FOUR

Ry-Gaul, Solace, and Clive shot through the holographic portal in the tanglewoods of Bellassa. Ferus had contacted them, and they'd taken off from Coruscant within the hour.

Solace glanced at Ry-Gaul. She was no chatterbox, but Ry-Gaul was the most silent being she'd ever met. Since they'd found him on Coruscant, on the run from the Empire, he'd told his story briefly and then rarely ventured an opinion or observation. Solace didn't mind the quiet, but she knew it was driving Clive crazy. If she had a sense of humor, she'd find it funny. Luckily she didn't have the time or temperament to be amused.

"Hey, mates," Clive said. "We had to dodge ten Imperial patrols and a buzz droid or two, but looks like we made it. I say *whew*. Glad to be here. Don't all speak at once."

Solace kept her eyes on the console. "Look for that

landing site. I have the general coordinates, but they move the site for safety. We need a visual."

"There." Ry-Gaul's voice was low.

"He speaks," Clive muttered.

Solace saw it ahead. A scrim of bush and knotted tree trunks, but a clear space for a small craft to land. She eased the ship inside.

They scrambled out of the cockpit hatch. Someone stepped out of the tangle of underbrush and held up a hand. It was Ferus.

Their meetings were infrequent now that he was a double agent. Solace felt a rush of gladness at seeing him. Could it be she was actually starting to grow fond of him?

He walked toward them, and the pleasure she felt was suddenly invaded by unease. Something was wrong.

He nodded to Ry-Gaul. "I was overwhelmed when Solace told me you were alive. Every Jedi we find is a gift. To find someone I knew . . . someone I had mourned . . ." Ferus faltered. His eyes were wet.

"I remember you well," Ry-Gaul said. "I do not remember you this emotional."

"I've changed."

"We have all changed." It was the most Ry-Gaul had spoken in more than a day.

"Ferus, we're all sorry about Roan," Solace said. "He is one with the Force now."

"He was one of the best," Clive said. "The galaxy is diminished."

Ferus didn't acknowledge their comments. Again, the unease sent its tendrils snaking around Solace's insides. The Ferus she knew would have said something, would have agreed or shared how he was feeling.

"We can't risk a long communication, so Solace wasn't able to give me details," Ferus said, changing the subject abruptly back to Ry-Gaul. "How did you escape Order 66?"

"I was on a mission that only Yoda and Mace knew about," Ry-Gaul said. "I was undercover, not traveling as a Jedi. Some scientists took me in — a man and his wife. They disappeared, and I've been looking for them. Tobin Gantor and Linna Naltree."

"But Linna Naltree is here," Ferus said. "She's working for the Empire. Under duress, I think. She was the one who helped Trever escape the garrison when Amie was captured and . . ." Ferus stopped. He swallowed.

He can't even speak Roan's name, Solace realized.

"Can we get her out?" Ry-Gaul asked.

"I don't know," Ferus said. "I don't know what pressure Vader is putting on her. I can try to talk to her."

Ry-Gaul exhaled. "I'm glad she's here and not in some prison. That was what I feared. As I searched, I found other scientists who had disappeared."

Ferus nodded. "They've been recruited by the

25

Empire for a big project. I just don't know what it is. Only the Emperor, Vader, and maybe Moff Tarkin know the extent of it. They're doing research, building something big. Maybe they're creating a whole prefabricated city and will plunk it down somewhere. Sounds crazy, but the plans are on that scale."

"So what's the plan to rescue Amie?" Solace asked. She pushed away her uneasiness. What was it, anyway? Something in his eyes? Some disturbance in the Force? Something about the way he wasn't really looking at her?

"We'll go over it after I get you into the city," Ferus said. "The Eleven sent a team to complete a tunnel under the lake near the landing platform. You'll have surprise on your side." Ferus hesitated. "I can't tell you how much I wish I could go on this mission with you."

"Nonsense," Solace said briskly. "We have you deep in Imperial territory. We can't pull you out for this."

"I'm scheduled to meet with Hydra, the Head Inquisitor, on Coruscant," Ferus said. "I'll have access to the list of possible Jedi. This means we could find others. In any case, I'll be far away when the plan is executed."

"Darth Vader will try to blame you anyway," Clive said. "He's nasty that way." Clive's dark eyes suddenly had a hint of sorrow in them. "But you are well acquainted with his ruthlessness," he said quietly.

It was the second acknowledgment Clive had made

of Ferus's pain, and Solace expected Ferus to turn to Clive, to let him know in word or gesture that he had heard it. But he didn't.

Instead, she felt the tremor in the Force that was surrounding Ferus. Vader's name had done it.

"We can use my transport to enter the city," Ferus said. "This vehicle has automatic clearance through the checkpoints."

"Too bad we can't use this baby on our getaway," Clive said, eyeing the airspeeder.

"All automatic clearances are canceled when an attack occurs," Ferus reported. "You wouldn't get far. We've got the checkpoints covered another way."

"Have you seen Vader since you were released from the holding cell?" Solace asked. She wasn't interested in the answer so much as Ferus's reaction to the name.

Ferus's face tightened. "He left the garrison for the mountains," he said.

Solace felt it again. The dark side of the Force was touching Ferus like a shadow. She wanted to tell him to beware, but this wasn't the time or place.

"I have to return to the garrison now," he said. "I'll drop you near the safe house. I don't want to bring an Imperial vehicle too close to it."

He was lying. She knew it. She didn't know why. Perhaps it was a harmless untruth, but Ferus had never told her a lie before.

They climbed into the transport. Ferus took off,

piloting the craft expertly through the crowded space lanes and zooming past the checkpoints. He dropped Solace, Clive, and Ry-Gaul at a deserted corner.

"May the Force be with you, Ferus," Solace said. She put layers of meaning into her words.

"I'll see you on Coruscant," he answered, turning away from her concern.

Then he headed off.

"I'll scout around," Clive said. "Make sure we weren't followed before we head to the safe house."

As soon as Clive left, Ry-Gaul spoke. "Are you sure of Ferus?" he asked.

"Yesterday I would have said yes," Solace said. "But I feel it, too. Something has happened to him since Roan died. The Emperor released him from that cell. Even after he attacked Vader."

Ry-Gaul's eyes were silver in the dying light. "I felt the dark side of the Force. Just a vibration, nothing more."

"We have all been tempted by anger," Solace said. "He has lost his partner. Someone who was closer than anyone else to him."

"So he is struggling now with grief," Ry-Gaul said. "The danger, of course, is if his grief turns to anger."

"His better nature will win," Solace said. "The Force is strong in Ferus. He will remember the Jedi way."

Ry-Gaul looked around as the shadows lengthened around them. "It is a new galaxy," he said.

It was a remark Solace was beginning to understand was typical of Ry-Gaul. It seemed merely an observation. Yet it said so much more.

In this new galaxy controlled by the Empire, shadows were deeper. There were caverns to fall into, very deep holes, treacherous places where even the best of beings could become lost. People could turn. No wonder when they saw each other they spoke so much of being changed. They had changed, and kept on changing; they were hard and getting harder. Their rage and sorrow could tip them into a place the dark side of the Force could reach.

Not Ferus, Solace said to herself. *It will never happen to Ferus.*

CHAPTER FIVE

Ferus had felt Solace's worry. He should have been better at concealment. He would have to learn that. He imagined that Palpatine was a master at it. He'd fooled an entire Senate, after all. Not to mention the Jedi Council.

The memory of what he had done at the garrison still weighed heavily on him. He'd been afraid Solace would pick up on it — and she had.

He had lied to her, too. He wasn't going back to the garrison. He couldn't bear to tell them where he was going, because he couldn't bear to say Roan's name in front of them. That was when the anger rose up and choked him.

There was one more thing he had to do before he left Bellassa. He had to pay a visit to Roan's family.

Once they had been his family, too. Ferus had arrived on Bellassa friendless and alone. He had lived all his life in the Jedi Temple. There had been plenty of contemplation and solitude there, but you were always surrounded by the humming life and energy of the place. You felt connected. When he'd come to Ussa he'd felt as though gravity was no longer working for him, that he was simply floating through space and time, not connecting to anyone or anything. Then Roan had befriended him and grounded him. He'd brought him home.

Ferus was careful to leave the Imperial speeder at a checkpoint and take a long walk to Roan's parents. They were living in a different home now, under another name. It had become too dangerous for them to live openly as Roan's family. Roan had restricted his visits in the last year. Ferus hadn't seen them at all.

He stood in front of the door, knowing that the sensor was checking him out for weapons. His lightsaber would be picked up and an alert would go off inside. But they would recognize him and let him in.

The door opened. Roan's mother, Enna, put out her hand. Tears glittered in her eyes. "Ferus. You came."

He stepped into her embrace. "I had to."

She drew him inside. She put a hand on his cheek. "Thank you."

He followed her into the main room. Roan's father, Alexir, stood and hugged him. "Thank you for coming." His voice was hoarse.

Feelings surged through Ferus, making him disoriented. He felt like a clumsy protocol droid with a bad servomotor, stumbling about the room greeting Roan's close friends and family who had gathered in the Bellassan tradition of Nine Days of Mourning. No one would leave Alexir and Enna's house until the nine days were up, and then the group would rotate visits for nine weeks. Ferus knew the tradition well. He had participated in it himself three years before when Roan's beloved Aunt Lilia had died.

Ferus sat next to Enna. This was tradition, too. The latest to arrive always took a seat next to the mother.

"Now the family is complete," Enna said.

Alexir turned to Ferus. "Tell us," he said. "We know only that he died in the garrison."

This was what he had come for, but Ferus couldn't find the words.

Enna looked him in the eyes, reassuring him with her gaze. "You must tell us everything."

He knew they would blame him. But he owed them the truth. It was why he had come. It was why he'd been afraid to come.

"Roan volunteered for the mission. A team went into the garrison to break into the computers to discover what the Imperials are really doing in the factories. We were discovered. Darth Vader appeared. I arrived — Darth Vader would assume I was on his side. You know . . . I am working for the Empire now. At least, it appears that way."

"Roan told us everything on his last visit," Enna

said, touching his arm. "We never believed you were truly working for them."

Ferus cleared his throat. He didn't feel worthy of the trust and affection in this room. It should be Roan who was here. He was a poor substitute for their son, and yet they were so kind they would die before they let him feel it.

"I was talking to him, trying to persuade him to release Roan and Amie into my care. I was in the middle of a sentence, in the middle of a *word*. There was no warning. One moment Vader was standing there, the next moment his lightsaber . . ." Ferus stopped as he felt Enna flinch.

"Roan was struck down," Ferus continued, forcing the words through his constricted throat. "I knelt with him. His last message to me was to stay silent, not to avenge him. His last thought was not for himself."

He felt Enna's deep shudder.

"I should have known Vader would strike," Ferus said.

"You couldn't know," Alexir assured him.

"We're glad you were with him," Enna said. "He would have wanted you to be with him. That will give me comfort always."

They didn't blame him. They included him in their sorrow. Ferus felt he might break down. He got up quickly and left the room.

He blundered into the kitchen. Covered dishes lined

the counters. The larder was full . . . food brought to grieving relatives. It was a custom throughout the galaxy. *What purpose did it serve?* he wondered. It was a ritual for the givers, he imagined, not those who sat with their grief hour after hour. Nothing would help them.

He had brought nothing except the details of death to this house.

He would walk away from all this sorrow and know he was responsible for it. Of course they had told him he couldn't have anticipated Vader's move. They didn't understand the Jedi. They didn't know that any Jedi worth his or her training would have anticipated it.

Ferus slammed his fist down on the counter.

"Don't break Enna's dishes," a voice said behind him. "You know how she feels about them."

He turned. It took him a minute to recognize who had spoken. "Malory?"

"It's me." She gave a small smile. "A little changed from when you last saw me."

It had been at her mother's Nine Days of Mourning. Malory was Lilia's daughter, Roan's first cousin. He remembered her as a young girl, slender and pale, with long silky hair the color of moonlight. Now her hair was cropped short and she looked more mature, meeting his glance with a direct friendly gaze that reminded him suddenly of Roan. A fresh pain sliced through him.

"I'm so sorry about Roan," she said. "I don't have any words for you. There are none."

34

The simple words touched him, and he wanted to turn away to hide it, but he didn't. "I know."

Malory moved to the counter and began to make tea. Ferus sat, admiring her sensitivity. She was giving him a moment to recover.

"What have you been doing these past few years?" he asked.

"I was a med student on Coruscant," she said. "Got through all my training during the Clone Wars. I trained at ChanPal."

Ferus nodded. ChanPal was the hospital facility in Galactic City that was renowned as one of the best in the galaxy.

"Then the Emperor took over the facility." Malory made a face as she reached for a tray. "At first it wasn't so bad, but now . . ." She shrugged. "It's called EmPal SuRecon now — Emperor's Surgical Reconstruction Center. We started turning away non-human patients. The best doctors and personnel started to quit, and they recruited others. When I finished my training they offered me a job, but I said no. I won't work for the Empire. So I left and came back home. I'm needed here more, anyway."

She placed the teapot and mugs on the tray. Ferus had been half-listening to her, but something pinged among the clutter of words. He reached for it.

He heard Palpatine's voice in his head. *I created him.*

Vader's body armor, his breath-mask, his helmet.

Could it be that Vader received his state-of-the-art prosthetics at the Emperor's pet project?

Malory hoisted the tray.

"Wait," Ferus said.

"Would you like some tea?" Malory asked politely.

"No," Ferus said. "But I would like your help."

"Name it. You're family."

"I need you to take that job at EmPal."

Carefully, Malory put down the tray. "Ferus, ask me anything, but don't ask me to do that."

"It's about avenging Roan's death," Ferus said.

Her gaze was steady on him, reading him. She took a breath. "Then I'm in."

CHAPTER SIX

Jenna Zan Arbor was making Darth Vader wait. No doubt it was a ploy of some kind. She didn't know how irritable he was when beings thought they could manipulate him. She'd learn.

He had come down to the hangar as a mark of respect he didn't have but wanted to demonstrate. The ship had landed, but she had not emerged. He would think that she would be more mindful of the respect owed to him. Not to mention the fact that she was hoping to land a contract with the Empire.

What she didn't know was that he needed her more than she needed him. Which was why he was still standing here.

The air in the mountains was thin and sharp. A raw wind blew the top layer of snow into the air, icy particles that bit into exposed skin. Another storm was on the way. Vader knew the troops and officers weren't happy about leaving the relative comforts of Ussa. They didn't like the treacherous mountain terrain or the way the locals kept obscuring trails or building traps for their airspeeders. The Dark Lord ignored the complaints. The mountains had become a refuge for the Eleven. There were hundreds of resistors holed up here. The place must be purged.

He was a second away from leaving when Jenna Zan Arbor appeared at the top of the ramp, dressed in a metallic leathris cloak with black feathers, her still-blond hair piled high in a ridiculous coiffure. She paused, for effect. Was he supposed to admire her? He supposed she had been beautiful in her day, but that was long ago. Surgeries and treatments had kept her skin smooth and tight, but she was a human woman, after all. The life she had lived may not have showed in wrinkles or sags, but somehow the corruption inside her was evident.

And what will you look like, twenty years on?

The jolt of the voice rose in his mind. He felt heat rise inside his body armor. That voice — he must banish it. Forever. It was the voice of Padmé. It was the voice he heard in the middle of the night, awake and sleeping. It was what pushed him from his uneasy rest and led him to stalk the confines of the garrison, checking up on those who were working through the night, becoming the bane of the night shift.

It was why Ferus Olin had grown from a petty nuisance to a problem. It wasn't Ferus so much — he was insignificant — but the memories that leaked in when he was around. Looking at Ferus reminded Darth Vader of Anakin Skywalker. Before Ferus he had been able to think of Anakin as another person entirely.

He had derived so much satisfaction from killing Roan Lands. He hadn't planned it, but the opportunity had presented itself, and it had been the perfect solution. He had taken from Ferus what had been taken from him. He had vanquished his enemy and brought him down.

It had been so easy. He had felt so satisfied.

His nights, however, had not been easy.

Then the Emperor had stepped in. It had been a surprise, to say the least, that his Master had arranged for Ferus's release. Had even given him a new assignment. Vader still didn't know why. It could be simply a test for him, Ferus a puppet in his Master's hands. But Ferus's release had enraged him, and that had helped him restore his balance. His fever of anger was back to ice. He was in control now.

Except for the nights.

The thing to do was focus on the moment. He watched Zan Arbor descend the ramp. She had the same brittle vitality she'd had when he'd known her before. He'd met her when he'd been a Jedi apprentice. She'd been a galactic criminal then. He'd tracked her through the galaxy, had caught her. But she wouldn't recognize him now.

He didn't want to think of Obi-Wan Kenobi. He didn't want to think of Anakin Skywalker. He could not function if this woman reminded him of the past. No matter how much he needed her, he would send her away if that were the case.

With an effort of will, he chased away the ghosts of his past.

"Lord Vader." She stopped and bowed. "I didn't realize I had the honor of your personal reception. I would have emerged sooner."

"Do not start our acquaintance with a lie," Vader said.

For a moment, she was taken aback. Then she smiled. "All right. I made you wait to establish power. It's something I'm in the habit of doing. From now on, let us agree to be honest throughout our dealings. It is more efficient."

"Precisely." He knew she would lie anyway, but they might as well have the fiction that they trusted each other.

They walked into his private office, which was constantly monitored for bugging devices. No one could ever find out what he was about to do.

She settled herself in a chair, arranging her cloak in folds around her. "Now," she said, "I know the Empire is interested in weapon delivery systems on a massive scale. It's not my area of expertise, but —"

"That's not why you're here."

"Ah. Then what is the reason?"

"Rumors have reached me about a new drug you are

working on," Vader said. "You are close to perfecting an agent that can target specific areas of the brain."

"Yes. A memory agent. It can scan for memory and erase specific areas. It is related to time. In other words, I should be able to blot out a week, or a month, or even years, if need be. I've discovered that there are timelines in the brain, timelines that can be mapped. . . . It is very technical."

"Have you tested the drug on humans?"

She shifted her position in the chair. "Only a few. It is difficult . . . to get human subjects. That's why I placed the request to the Emperor for access to prisoners."

"I can obtain for you human subjects," Vader said curtly. "That is not a problem. As well as funding, and technical help."

"The human subjects . . . yes, I need them, but not just anyone," Zan Arbor said. "To be able to pinpoint timelines can be confusing if there is too much experience. In these early stages, I need to start on . . . more impressionable subjects. With limited experience."

"I see. I can arrange that," Vader said. "And in return . . ."

She waited, her blue eyes alert. She knew there would be a deal that had to be struck.

"You must, of course, sign away all rights to the procedure, ceding them to the Empire. "

Zan Arbor shook her head. "I have never signed over the rights to my work. It is my integrity."

He had expected this. It was part of the negotiation.

"Nevertheless, I must insist." He let a moment pass. "Aside from the benefits of not turning down a request from the Empire . . ." He let his words trail off, let her munch on the implications of this. She swallowed. Vader continued. ". . . we can work out the necessary financial arrangements so that you will reap the benefits if the procedure is successful. We are less interested in profits than the use of your discovery."

She let that sink in. He knew her greed. As long as she was guaranteed profits, she would sign over anything.

"Assuming we can come to a financial agreement," she said, "there are some other things I would want."

He waved a gloved hand for her to continue.

"An apartment in the Republica 500 tower."

The tower that the Emperor used for his private quarters. The apartments were luxurious, difficult to get, Senators jockeying, bribing, to get one. Lifelong feuds had begun over the competition for those apartments.

"Done," Vader said.

"On a high floor!" she warned. "Also, a personal introduction to Raith Sienar, and a starship designed by him, retrofitted to my personal specifications. Paid for by the Empire."

"Agreed."

"A high-level security pass so I don't have to stop for security checks anywhere in the galaxy. It is so time-consuming."

A right awarded only to the highest level of officials, such as himself or Moff Tarkin — soon to be Grand Moff.

"Agreed."

She looked startled, then crafty. He knew she was surprised at how easily he had acquiesced to those things and was trying to think of more to ask for.

"So we have a deal." He said this flatly, warning her that she shouldn't go on.

"Pending the financial agreement, yes."

Something inside him relaxed. If she succeeded, if he was certain her procedure was foolproof, he had a way out of his nightmares.

Padmé would be gone.

Anakin Skywalker would be gone.

They would just be names he would hear in passing. They would make no impression on him. If his Master reminded him, which sometimes he liked to do, to test him and torment him, he would hear that he had once loved someone and it would mean nothing to him.

Padmé, you will be just a name to me. Nothing more. And that is all you deserve because of your betrayal!

He wrenched his attention back to Zan Arbor. "I have arranged for you to have an assistant. Linna

Naltree has trained at the best scientific institutes. She has extensive experience in neural studies. You both can work in the Imperial labs on Coruscant."

"And the human subjects?"

"I will send them shortly."

CHAPTER SEVEN

Volunteers from the Eleven had set up shifts and worked through two nights on the tunnel. It had been a dangerous job. Imperial patrols moved around Moonstone Lake in random patterns and times. The cold lake water required special suits, and the volunteers had to stay underwater for long periods. In the end, the volunteers couldn't guarantee the tunnel was completely watertight, but they were able to add enough meters to get close to the hangar itself.

Solace, Ry-Gaul, and Clive found the entrance cleverly hidden in the rocks, behind a holographic portal. The trio crawled inside the small opening and then continued to crawl into the tunnel.

"This is fun," Clive remarked, wrist deep in mud as he moved along. "Remind me to thank Ferus for this."

Ry-Gaul said nothing, of course. He was a tall man, and yet he seemed to move with great ease through the mud, even on his hands and knees. Solace was already twenty meters ahead.

Clive sighed. What was he doing here anyway, slogging through mud underneath a half-frozen lake? He was no Jedi. He didn't have the mind control to pretend he wasn't in pain. Freezing water dripped through the makeshift tunnel onto his head. It snaked down the neck of his tunic. He'd thought nothing could be worse than an Imperial prison.

Okay, this might be worse, he admitted to himself.

Why was this always happening to him? He had resolved to stay neutral in the Clone Wars, and he'd wound up a double agent. Well, at least he'd done that for the credits that were shoved his way. But here he was, involved in the resistance on a planet that wasn't even his homeworld, working with two Jedi he barely knew while his pal Ferus was off hobnobbing with the Emperor's favorites!

At first he'd thought it would be a lark to help out Ferus. And, well, he'd had nothing better to do. He'd expected to be hiding out in some cushy joint and waiting out the Empire. It had to fall sooner or later. Why did he have to get involved in giving it a push? He had actually *volunteered* for this.

He would have to revisit his stand on loyalty. That was it. He owed Ferus a favor, and fell in with Ferus's mates, and they had taken him in, so he'd figured he owed them. And he did. But how much? Did that include getting on his hands and knees in mud and crawling toward heavily armed stormtroopers?

With every gain in forward movement, the water rose. Soon they were slogging through a half-meter of cold lake . . . and it was still rising. The plastoid above his head was starting to crack.

The lake was so large it had tides. Had anyone investigated that? What if the tide came in?

With such thoughts for company, Clive was surprised when Solace stopped moving and held up a hand to stop. The ceiling of the tunnel was now only centimeters over his head. He was almost flat. If he laid down, he'd be underwater.

She signaled to them that they had reached the end of the tunnel. That meant they were squarely in Imperial territory.

They were right on schedule. And in his experience, the Empire's forces were usually right on the dot. He touched his utility belt to make sure his blaster was there. It was a nervous habit. He wasn't a shooting kind of guy; he preferred more unusual weaponry. Ry-Gaul and Solace had told him if all went according to plan, he wouldn't have to shoot at all.

In his experience, all *never* went according to plan.

His teeth began to chatter from cold and nerves. Clive clamped his jaw shut. Sometimes being brave was just doing what you said you'd do.

Solace held up five fingers. The countdown. That

meant that the stormtroopers had emerged with Amie and were leading her to the transport. He couldn't see a thing except the gleam of Solace's fingers and the blackness beyond.

Five
Four
Three
Two
One
Go!

He found he could move fast if he had to, but not as fast as Ry-Gaul and Solace. He scuttled forward, moving on his elbows now. Solace had disappeared into the blackness ahead. Then Ry-Gaul shot out of the opening. Clive pushed himself through.

He emerged on a rocky beach of black sand. The Jedi's eyes must have adjusted immediately, but it took him a few long moments to see through the early dawn and the streaking, icy rain. The outdoor landing platform glistened ahead. There were no lights on. He could barely make out some droid hover-loaders in inactive mode. It took him several blinks to see the figures walking quickly toward a black starship. Stormtroopers surrounded a slight figure, propelling her forward by her elbows. Sometimes her feet dragged and they yanked her up.

The stormtroopers hadn't seen Solace and Ry-Gaul yet. The Jedi were moving so quietly and so fast that

Clive could barely see them himself. His job was to stay out of the battle and snatch Amie.

Through the spitting rain he saw the spinning arc of lightsabers. Ry-Gaul raised a hand and an entire line of stormtroopers shot backward as though pushed by a turbodozer. He couldn't see Solace, just the tracing of light moving through the air as bodies slammed into pavement. Now streaks of blasterfire shattered the blackness like cracks on glass. All the while he was running, lungs aching. He could hear his panting breath.

He had seen Ferus use his lightsaber, but Clive felt a fresh sense of amazement at witnessing the two Jedi in action. It was perfect movement, perfect timing. For two Jedi who rarely strung a sentence together, they knew how to communicate. Ry-Gaul and Solace made taking down two squads of stormtroopers armed with blasters and grenades look easy.

It was all so fast. He knew they couldn't wait for him, but he was falling behind. Amie was in danger.

She must have faked her weakness, because suddenly she was running from her captors, diving and rolling under the starship ramp. Clive fumbled for his blaster but then it was in his hand as he dived underneath from the opposite end and found her. Her eyes were clear and determined, but he could also see her fear.

"You're supposed to come with me," he said.

This was the hard part. Trusting the Jedi. They had

told him he needed to run, to not think about the blasters at his back, that they'd protect him. He just needed to take Amie and go.

He wasn't good at trusting someone to watch his back, but Amie didn't seem to have the same problem. She nodded, and they ran, with Clive shielding her as best he could. They could hear the explosions behind them but they didn't turn. The permacrete was slick with rain but they flew over it, heading back down toward the lake's edge.

They were almost at the end of the permacrete when the security lights suddenly blazed on at full power. Clive heard the rapid fire of an E-Web repeating blaster, which was definitely something you didn't want to hear at your back.

"Jump!" he cried. They jumped down the slope to the beach, rolling into darkness. Clive got a mouthful of sand.

He came up spitting and cursing. He helped Amie up and they raced along the beach. He knew any moment there would be searchlights sweeping the area, but they didn't have far to go. Amie was starting to gasp, and she held her side.

"Almost there," he grunted.

The Eleven had prepared one more surprise — another portal, this one hidden in the rocky hillside that rose to the cliff overlooking the lake. He saw Dona rise from the wet rocks like a seal. She beckoned to them.

They made it inside the portal as the searchlights blazed and swept the shoreline. They burrowed into the trail in the rocks, moving fast. The passage was cleverly concealed, with rocks and seaweed layered over it so it would be invisible from the air. At times they had to crawl, but they were able to make it up the cliff without being spotted.

They got to the top and came out at a small parking area for airspeeders. This overlook had once been a popular spot but had fallen into disrepair with the coming of the Empire's battalion.

Dona's gray hair was plaited down her back. She was dressed as an Ussan priest, the ones who brought bodies to burial and drove white carts pulled by native beasts called dhunas.

Amie let out a choked laugh. "This is my escape? Being dead?"

"You arguing? Go!"

Amie slipped into the white cart festooned with flowers. Dona quickly clapped down the board that covered the open back. She began to drive the dhuna forward with crooning noises that were like singing, the chants the priests made as they walked through the streets. She headed up the beach trail to the paved lane.

Clive ran along the permacrete, his lungs on fire. He had to loop around and come up through a wooded area into a main thoroughfare of the Moonstone District. He'd walked the route yesterday. If everything went according to plan, he'd find a member of the Eleven waiting for him.

They had all pitched in. Amie would be transferred from hand to hand, from cart to speeder to gravsled. The Jedi would follow. As Amie approached the safe house, the helpers would drop away until only the original team was left.

There were multiple checkpoints to pass through. Diversions to stage. It wasn't over yet. Even now the alarms were no doubt ringing in the Imperial garrisons all over the city.

Amie was free, but she wasn't safe. They still had a long way to go.

CHAPTER EIGHT

Trever found his way slowly to his piloting class. It turned out there were maps in central kiosks throughout the complex — only nobody had told him. Each map gave him small portions of the layout, so he was never quite sure if he was going in the right direction.

They didn't care about maps, but they managed to hang huge lasersigns reading SAFETY SECURITY JUSTICE PEACE on every major hallway. And holoprojections of the Emperor in better days, before his hideous scarring.

He hated this school. It was designed to humiliate and control. Well, of course it was. It was run by the Empire in order to fashion little Imperials who would become big moffing evildoing Imperials.

He made it to class with seconds to spare. To his dismay, Kestrel was there, the student who was supposed to be his advisor, but whom he was perfectly certain would turn out to be his tormentor. Kestrel stood at the front, talking to the instructor, who turned out to be Lieutenant Maggis.

Thanks for the directions, sir.

Kestrel saw Trever and flashed a cocky grin. He threaded through the other students and came toward him.

"Hey, Fortin. Fifteen degrades on your first day. Not exactly a stellar beginning."

"I'm not worried," Trever said.

"You should be," Kestrel replied, putting his hand on his fake blaster. "I just might decide to give you another."

Trever was about to blow everything and tell Kestrel what he really thought when he spotted Lune across the room. That gave him the self-control he needed. He thought of Ferus, deep in enemy territory. He began to understand now what kind of self-control Ferus must have to exercise in order to make it through a single day.

Lune was much younger than he was, so he was surprised to see that they were in the same class. But he should have guessed that the kid's Force-ability would land him in advanced piloting.

Maggis called the class to order, distracting Kestrel. Trever moved toward Lune. The boy hadn't seen him yet, and he didn't want Lune to betray him by looking surprised or calling out.

Instead, Lune surprised him. Of course the kid did. He was close to spooky, the way he could tell when someone was behind him. The Jedi Master Garen Muln had worked with him on "awareness tactics" back when they were all on the asteroid. Garen was practically a ghost now, his powers diminished, but he was still a good teacher. Trever wanted to think "awareness tactics" was just Jedi mumba-humba, but it actually did seem to work.

"Tell my mother I'm okay," Lune said without turning around, as soon as Trever was within earshot.

"Tell her yourself. I'm going to get you out of here," Trever replied.

Lune lifted a shoulder slightly, but Trever got the meaning: *Good luck.*

"Today, you worthless lunkheads, we're going to move on up to flight simulation," Maggis announced. "Note the key word, *simulation.* I wouldn't trust the lot of you to pilot me around a space park. Now pick a partner and decide who will be pilot and copilot without shooting each other and we'll begin."

It was lucky that Trever and Lune were standing together. As the new recruits, it was natural that they would pair up.

They made their way to one of the flight simulators and stepped inside the cockpit.

"I've got special handlers," Lune said once they were inside. "Spies that watch me. I think they report to Maggis. Kestrel is one. Him and his friend Flinn. I'm never alone."

"Not a problem," Trever said. "I've gotten out of worse places." He wasn't sure that was true, but it sounded good.

Lune took the pilot's seat and Trever swung into the copilot's. The cockpit window was a blank holographic screen. Suddenly it came alive with ships.

"You're in the middle of a battle," Maggis's voice boomed out from the system speaker. "Red against blue. Pilots fly. Copilots engage the enemy."

Trever grabbed the laser cannon controls of their ARC-170.

"Visual sightings only," Maggis said, his voice booming through the cockpit comm. "No targeting computers in this exercise."

"This should be fun," Trever said.

He aimed the cannon at a nearby vessel, honing in on it.

"Trever, we're blue!" Lune shouted. "Shoot at the *red* guys!"

"Oops!" Trever swung the cannon around and aimed at a red ship on the monitor. He squeezed the trigger. The ship exploded on-screen.

"I am one full moon amazing shot!" Trever crowed.

"Watch out, Captain Amazing, there's one coming up on our left," Lune said, diving the craft down.

The battle program was complicated and fast. In addition to competing against the other students, they had other obstacles to contend with. It was a large-scale battle, and Star Destroyers and Tri-Fighters would suddenly enter the airspace. Buzz droids would suddenly loom. Asteroids careened toward them. Trever had a fine time blasting away at the other starfighters, but he knew he wouldn't have lasted a minute without Lune at the helm. The boy seemed to know when a zoomy ARC-170 would dog their tail before it registered on the screen.

One by one, the other flight simulator teams were blasted out of the sky. Soon only Trever and Lune were left with Kestrel and his partner, Flinn.

"I think we should let them win," Lune muttered as put the ship into a steep climb. "We don't want to attract too much attention."

Trever took a moment to shoot a look at Lune. "Or we could just win and drive Kestrel crazy."

Lune grinned.

Kestrel was a good pilot, but Lune was better. Lune stayed above them, flying fast, as fast as the simulator would go, and never lost control. He let them chase him. The program released a field of asteroids into the frame. Lune dodged them easily. One of them clipped one of Kestrel's wings.

"That's it. He's going to have control problems. I'm going in," Lune murmured. "Get ready."

Trever hunched over the controls. "Go."

Lune was calm as he swept the ship into an arc. Then he suddenly heeled to the right and dived. "I'll tell you when to shoot."

Trever would have been annoyed, but he knew Lune's skill was greater than his own.

"Now. Starboard guns."

Trever shot the starboard laser cannons and Lune made a sharp starboard turn. It seemed simultaneous, which would make the aim go awry, but it was a split second before, and the aim was true. Kestrel was already firing at them, but the fire streaked across open space. Trever's shot went home. Kestrel's ship exploded.

Trever let out a whoop of pure joy. The class cheered and jeered, depending on their loyalties. Kestrel had his supporters, but most of the younger recruits had been rooting for Lune and Trever.

They climbed out of the cockpit simulator. Kestrel's neck was bright red as he climbed out at the same time. *Oops*, Trever thought. They'd humiliated him. They were fresh recruits, and they'd beaten him.

Squ-awk! Ruby-throated kete! Trever wanted to cat-call, but he bit back the insult.

Maggis called for attention. "That was the most pathetic display I've ever seen," he said in disgust. "I've seen toddlers in a nursery throw blocks with more accuracy. All of you should be flunked out today. Divinian, you were the only one to show any skill whatsoever. Fortin, you get a failing grade."

"But I blasted Kestrel out of the sky!" Trever protested.

"I heard that yell. You showed emotion. That's

against Imperial rules. Do that in a cockpit again and the next thing you know you'll be eating slop on a tray in the Mining Corps."

Kestrel smirked at him.

"Tomorrow we take a look at some real starships in the hangar, so I want you up on your manuals. Strain your puny brains. Class dismissed. In other words, get out of my sight."

The class started to move out as the clanging bells and flashing lights urged them to hurry.

Kestrel drifted behind them.

"You're going down, Fortin," he said.

"You think? Seems like you're the one who just flamed out," Lune replied.

"I wouldn't make friends with Fortin if I were you, Divinian," Flinn said, coming up close to Lune's side and leaning in. "He's not going to last long. Pretty soon he'll be a drone worker on a mining planet."

"Maybe," Trever said. "But I know one thing for sure — we just outflew you, outgunned you, and out-classed you."

Kestrel opened his mouth angrily, but just then they passed under the gaze of Maggis, who stood at the door-way, arms folded. He looked at them from under his heavy black brows.

"That probably wasn't the best move," Trever mut-tered as they entered the swirl of recruits in the hallway. "It was the stupidest thing we could have done."

"Yeah," Lune said cheerfully. "But it sure felt good."

Trever looked over his shoulder. Maggis was still watching them.

"I'd better take off. Don't think we should be seen together. As soon as I come up with a plan, I'll find you."

"I already have a plan," Lune said. "Meet me in the commons room an hour after lights-down tonight."

CHAPTER NINE

Ferus was desperate for news, but he was traveling with a group of Imperial officers and couldn't show his agitation by the tiniest look or gesture. He knew that the operation on Ussa should have been completed by now. Amie should be at the Eleven's safe house. But the coded signal hadn't been sent. Something must have gone wrong.

The Imperial ship dipped into the inner atmosphere of Coruscant. They headed for the busy high-clearance Imperial landing stage. Ferus wasn't used to arriving on Coruscant so officially. He'd had to sneak to and from the planet several times, and it hadn't been easy. Now clearances were completed in minutes, and soon he was ushered into a luxurious airspeeder and taken directly to one of the private small landing platforms at the Senate complex. There a military escort greeted him and ushered him to the office of the Inquisitors, several levels down from Palpatine's office in the Senate Tower.

The sergeant left him at Hydra's office door. She waved her hand over the sensor for him before pivoting and marching off.

A short, slender humanoid rose as Ferus walked in. He couldn't tell if Hydra was male or female, but he guessed she was a female. He couldn't guess at her homeworld. A hood covered her head and she wore the enveloping dark maroon of the Inquisitor team, the color that always reminded Ferus of dark blood. Her eyes were a pale silver color. She tipped back the hood and her shiny skull shone through a light stubble of hair. Her voice was husky. "Emperor Palpatine has directed me to be at your service."

Ferus inclined his head.

"You are to be in charge of the search for Force-adepts. We have made progress. I have a list of possibles for you. You may use my dataport." Hydra stiffly lifted an arm and pointed to a console. "I have already entered my password."

Ferus nodded. "I'd like to get started as soon as possible."

"Then begin."

Ferus sat at the console. The database had already been loaded. He scrolled through it.

"You'll see it has been ranked in terms of importance."

Number one was a "tall human male, silver hair, large build, homeworld unknown," who had slipped through a stormtrooper snare only a week before. Ry-Gaul. Ferus suddenly felt better. They'd actually tracked a Jedi. Maybe this list would prove valuable. He could help Ry-Gaul, set the Empire off on a false trail that would allow Ry-Gaul a chance to disappear completely.

Ferus went through the list. Some of the reports looked promising. A pilot in the Mid-Rim who made freight runs to the Core and made several extraordinary escapes from Imperial tails. A teacher who had single-handedly saved a school full of children from a sudden groundquake with such skill and speed that it had attracted attention. A bounty hunter. An account of a toddler on Alderaan who had seemed to sense danger before it happened, saving her minder. Sounded like a coincidence to Ferus. He ranked it last. The pilot, the teacher, and the bounty hunter all sounded promising.

The thought that any of them could be Jedi was the first ray of light in the dark days since Roan's death.

"I'll study this and get back to you with priorities," Ferus said. "We'll need a starship with a hyperdrive."

"Already requisitioned. I will be accompanying you."

Lucky me, Ferus thought. Hydra made the former Head Inquisitor Malorum look like the life of the party.

Hydra wanted to leave immediately, but Ferus managed to put off the trip until the next day, claiming he needed to do additional research.

At last he was free of the Empire.

With his credentials, Ferus moved easily through the checkpoints of the Senate complex. He passed through the entrance to EmPal and found Malory Lands waiting for him in the reception area. She was dressed in the white scrubs that all med personnel wore.

"Looks like you got a job," Ferus said.

"Wasn't hard," she answered. "Follow me."

She led him through a maze of hallways, passing closed door after closed door. Finally she reached one marked RADIATION UNIT. She handed Ferus some protective clothing, and he slipped it on.

Inside, the room hummed with machinery. A large transparisteel chamber stood in the center, surrounded by dataports and screens. "Advanced therapy for post-surgical procedures," Malory explained. "The machines in here are highly calibrated. Any surveillance equipment would cause fused circuits and severe breakdowns. This is the only place I know where it's safe to talk."

"Is the entire place under surveillance?"

"I don't think so, but main areas are monitored," she said. "This is just a precaution. There are patrolling surveillance droids, but they're supposedly for security. It's mostly a rumor among the staff. They say there's no such thing as a private conversation. I think it's more likely that there are spies among them who get rewards for reporting back to the managers. Hard to tell, so far." She shrugged. "Most med centers are rumor mills. No exception here. There's even a rumor about a ghost. I can see why — this place is creepy." She grinned, and for a moment Ferus saw the young woman inside the crisp professional.

"Can you give me access to records?"

"We're in luck. All the record offices are fully staffed during the day, so there's never really a chance to be in there alone. But . . . there's a technician on the night shift named Jako. He's going to be fired soon, he just doesn't know it. He keeps getting partners, they keep requesting transfers, or they quit. I'm friends with the employment director — told her my cousin needs a job. So you're in. You can bluff your way through with Jako. He's not very bright."

"Can we do it tonight?"

"Sure. Just do me a favor. Don't get caught. There are rumors of medics who've disappeared. I don't mind helping you, Ferus, but I'd like to stay healthy."

Ferus looked at Malory, with her gaze so like Roan's, and spoke the truth. "I won't let anything happen to you. I'd die first."

She grinned, and the flash of Roan hit him again. "Just so I'm not second."

CHAPTER TEN

Ussans always began their workday early, in darkness, so that they could quit in late afternoon in order to take advantage of the long late afternoon light. In Ussa, twilight was called "the endless hour." That was when families crowded the cafés and children played in the parks. Back in the time every Ussan could still remember, before the Empire came.

Before sunrise, they were crowding the streets and space lanes with airspeeders, packing the buses, and hurrying along the broad walkways. This crush was a crucial element in the plan to rescue Amie.

All members of the Eleven had spread the word. Even to those without jobs. And to the airbus drivers, the air taxis, the pedestrians. *Flood the streets and space lanes*, they'd said. *Create traffic, maybe an accident or two. Or three.* But they had to be careful. It had to look natural. They could not risk their children again.

Many were reluctant, especially those whose children

had been taken only the week before. But the power of the Eleven and a personal appeal from Wil swayed them to the cause.

Clive had heard of the now-legendary cooperation of the Bellassan people. He knew that almost every citizen supported the Eleven. It was one reason why Ferus had been able to operate so long. No one betrayed him. No spies could be recruited by the Empire. But he had to admit he had cast a cynical eye on the Bellassan resistance from a distance. In his experience, beings could be noble, but only up to a point. Self-interest would always win out.

So he was stunned when the citizens of Ussa risked everything and took to the streets.

The crush of traffic was the perfect cover. Checkpoints were overwhelmed. Airspeeders idled, airbuses broke down. Pedestrians milled in small crowds, spreading into the lanes for wheeled traffic. And in the confusion, Amie was passed from vehicle to vehicle.

At the checkpoints, the stormtroopers couldn't handle the mass, so random gravsleds and airspeeders were able to break through and disappear into the chaos on the other side or down alleys that ran behind many of the twisting streets. Soon the garrisons sent out more stormtroopers, but it would take time before the city could be managed.

Clive's job was simply to keep Amie in sight and try to add to the chaos. He did his part, piloting an airspeeder and then abandoning it to block a lane, jumping aboard a gravsled and taking it through the back alleys to keep Amie in sight, who was now aboard a different speeder. Her last ride was with Dona again, this time in a utility skiff that the Eleven had blastproofed and secretly tweaked to give it advanced speed and agility.

All the while, more and more patrols appeared. The skylanes were now thick with prowler vehicles trying to get a lock on Amie's position. But even the dreaded prowlers were having a hard time distinguishing between the vehicles and pedestrians jamming the streets.

They were almost to the last checkpoint. This would be the tricky part. No question. Clive knew the Jedi must be around him somewhere, but they were gleaming good at concealing themselves when they had to.

On foot now, he slowed to a walk. He could see Dona ahead at the checkpoint, several vehicles back in line. Wil was assigned the job of creating the diversion. Suddenly a garbage scow overturned, spewing foul-smelling material into the street. Airspeeders collided, an airbus let out all its passengers, and pedestrians ran from the garbage straight toward the checkpoint. At the same time Dona backed up her skiff, maneuvered around the checkpoint, and then zoomed forward.

She would have made it. As far as Clive could tell, everything had gone according to plan. But they couldn't plan for everything. They couldn't plan around the airspeeder full of stormtroopers that had been sent for reinforcements.

The airspeeder took off after Dona.

Clive was on foot. No one in line had reacted to the chase. The checkpoint line still moved. He flashed his ID docs and moved through. Then he picked up his pace and quickly joined the pedestrian walkway. As soon as he was out of sight of the guards, he began to run.

Dona pulled over. She knew she'd be blasted out of the skylane if she didn't. She was far ahead of him, and he dodged pedestrians, trying to keep her in sight without being too obvious about it. He saw her hand over her ID docs. The stormtrooper ordered her out.

One stormtrooper began to call in the information, while two others went to the back of the skiff. Clive's stomach twisted as they flung aside the tarp, but Amie had been hidden more cleverly than that. They stood examining the various items on the skiff.

Clive was just deciding on his next move when a streak of blasterfire suddenly ripped across the front of the Imperial airspeeder. A stormtrooper sitting in the pilot seat was hit. The blast didn't kill him but it did stun him. He was knocked backward, his helmet striking the seat.

Flame emerged from the crowd. In a flying leap, she booted the stormtrooper out of the seat and swung herself in. The airspeeder shot forward, plowing down the two stormtroopers who were inspecting the back of the skiff.

As the first stormtrooper reached for his blaster, Flame vaulted over the back bed of the skiff and into the pilot seat. Dona jumped back aboard and the skiff took off. Blasterfire streaked through the air. Pedestrians flattened themselves on the roadway. Clive could see Ry-Gaul and Solace, concealed by the pileup of speeders, intercepting the fire with their lightsabers when they could.

The stormtroopers raced for their airspeeder. They ignored their injured comrade and jumped in.

Clive knew that the next move of the Jedi would be to engage the stormtroopers directly, probably through one of those Jedi Force–assisted giant leaps that would no doubt expose them to all and target them for a full-scale hunt.

He reached into his utility belt and withdrew two small objects. He threw them as hard as he could and watched in satisfaction as they hit the airspeeder's two exhaust pipes.

The repulsorlift engine fired, then died. The storm-trooper pounded on the control panel. The engine started up and died again.

Flame and Dona were well away by now. Clive reversed direction and then strolled down an intersecting boulevard. Amazing what some dried blumfruit strips and a little synthplaster could do. Bounce right into an exhaust and clog it just enough to stop an air-speeder from its needed acceleration boost. Who needed a blaster when you had good tools?

"She's hurt," Dona said.

Dona supported Flame as they staggered into the safe house. Amie hurried behind. The others crowded forward to ask questions, but Amie held up a hand.

"Stay back. I'm fine. Someone get me the med kit."

They all watched as Flame was lowered to the floor. She put her head back and closed her eyes. Once again Clive was jolted by a familiar feeling.

I've seen her before.

Amie administered bacta and a painkiller. "It's not bad," she told Flame. "You'll be feeling better in a minute or two."

Flame nodded, biting her lip.

Only now did Amie allow Wil to approach her. He held out his arms and she stepped into them.

"Flame, we owe you a debt," Wil said.

Without opening her eyes, Flame said, "Do you trust me now?"

"We trust you," Amie said.

But Clive still wasn't sure.

He had an itch. And when he had an itch, he scratched.

He knew he wouldn't get rid of this nagging feeling until he did some digging. Toma had been the one to bring Flame to their attention. He had known her back on their shared homeworld, Acherin.

Clive sighed. The last thing he wanted to do was take a side trip to a planet he'd heard was in the middle of a civil war. But it looked like that's where he was going.

CHAPTER ELEVEN

Ferus filed in with the rest of the workers on the late shift. He wore the white med tunic with his ID tags around his neck. No one gave him a second glance. Following Malory's description he made his way through the hallways to the door marked INFORMATION CENTER. He swept his card through the sensor and heard the click with relief. Malory had promised she could enable him to enter, and she'd come through.

He had received at last the all-clear code from Wil on Bellassa. Amie was safe. He only hoped there wouldn't be a massive retaliation from the Imperial governor.

Here on the night shift there wasn't much to do for the info tech workers, so it was lightly staffed. A doctor or med trainee might call on them to enter a patient, but EmPal no longer had an emergency unit that took in all Coruscant citizens in need of care. Instead, patients were admitted by physicians. The high costs limited those admissions to Senators and the rich corporate people who now clogged Imperial City.

A plump young man sat at the console, crunching his way through a meal of root chips and a pressed protein slider. "Hey, new guy," he said as Ferus walked in.

Ferus sat at the other chair. "Ty Ambler," he said, giving the name on his ID tag.

"Jakohaul Lessor," he replied. "Just call me Jako. You just lucked into the sweetest job at EmPal, buddy. Not much doing here."

"Suits me fine," Ferus said. "I'm allergic to hard work."

Jako chuckled. "Second that." He pushed the greasy plate toward Ferus. "Want a root chip?"

"No thanks. I need to familiarize myself with the system."

"Just don't go crazy. We like to take it easy in this department."

Ferus began to call up the database and flipped through it in a seemingly casual way. He zeroed in on records from the end of the Clone Wars, near the time that Darth Vader had first surfaced.

While Jako crunched beside him and called up a Podrace on his vidscreen, Ferus searched through the material. Nothing popped out at him. EmPal had been changing over from its old role as a medical center open to all to an exclusive med facility and biomechanical reconstruction center. He could find no record of extraordinary procedures or evidence of a cover-up. Then again, he hadn't expected this to be easy.

Jako finished his meal and pushed back his rolling chair to rest his feet on the console. He crossed his arms on his chest. Ferus hoped he would go to sleep. The next step was to go deeper into the system, looking for security codes he could break. But the system might send up alarms or flashes that Jako could see from his position.

"Listen, new guy, I'm going to take a snooze," Jako said. "Don't wake me up if work calls. And don't be scared of the ghost!" he chortled.

Ferus was relieved as Jako's eyes closed.

The ghost. Malory had mentioned it, too.

"What ghost?" he asked.

Jako's eyes flew open, but he didn't seem annoyed at being disturbed. "It happened about a year ago," he said, lowering his voice to a ragged whisper. "Near the very end of the Clone Wars. A scream was heard. A scream so terrible and so loud that it echoed throughout the building and made the sensors go crazy. It was said that one med worker lost his hearing. *Permanently.* The med workers searched and searched for the source of the sound, but there was . . . nothing. There was only a handful of patients at that time. It had seemed to come from everywhere and nowhere, but no patient had done it." Jako's voice had lowered to a whisper. "It was as though all the dead of the Clone Wars had screamed their death cries at the same time, then gone back to being dead."

Ferus knew that in his slightly incoherent way Jako was trying to spook him, and it had worked. Just not in the way he'd thought.

Jako winked. "Enjoy the night shift." He closed his eyes again, and, smiling, was asleep in seconds.

Ferus thought once more about Vader's prosthetics. They were extensive, from a breath-mask to vision enhancement to possible artificial limbs. He was fairly certain that Vader had at least one artificial hand. And he was regulated by what seemed to be a complex bio-system within that suit.

For the first time, Ferus wondered what awful injuries he must have sustained. What had *happened* to the guy?

He had been chasing the wrong idea. Vader, whoever he was, must have been in terrible pain.

Ferus turned back to his console. He dumped the med records he'd been searching. There would be no mention there, not even behind security shields. He was suddenly positive of that. Instead, he accessed the blueprints of the building.

Everywhere and nowhere.

His instincts had kicked in, and he knew he was right. Somewhere in this building, Darth Vader had been born.

CHAPTER TWELVE

Sano Sauro's career might be ruined, but it wasn't over. He still had favors to call in, and if Senators and functionaries thought he'd just go away, they had another thing coming. He had been close to power, and he would be again.

His office in the Senate, that grand chamber that had trumpeted his power to one and all . . . that was gone, given to the Senator of some big Core system who had rolled over for the Emperor and needed to be thanked. Sauro was stuck in a tiny office at the new Imperial Navy building. His job was to oversee the new Naval Academy. One school, in comparison to whole systems!

And, to make matters worse, those below him who had served him, fools who had done just what he wanted but had never been able to come up with an original plan on their own — fools like Bog Divinian — they were now Imperial governors. Wielding power without knowing what to do with it.

Sauro coughed in his handkerchief. The bile inside him was giving him trouble. His nights were restless, his days filled with bitterness. He had to get out of here. He had to rise again, and he had to wreak vengeance on those who had crossed him or, worse, patronized him.

His assistant, a dolt sent by the Imperial administration office, came in, looking nervous. "A communication for you, Lord Sauro."

"I'm not a lord. Call me Senator Sauro."

"But you're not a Senator . . . anymore."

"It doesn't matter!" Sauro snapped. "I still have the title!"

"Senator Sauro, a communication for you."

"Who is it? I'm busy."

"Lord Vader. He's a lord, isn't he?"

Sauro's eyes widened. "You left Lord Vader waiting? Put him through to my private holo-line immediately, you idiot!"

He was surrounded by fools.

He swiveled as the small holo-image surfaced on his desk.

"Greetings, Senator Sauro."

"It is an honor to —"

"I am running a project on a strictly 'need-to-know' basis. I am looking for a recruit at the Naval Academy to volunteer for the project."

"Of course, I'll arrange it right away. Any

requirements? Top of their class? Sons and daughters of those in favor?"

"No. Avoid those. And any children of Senators, anyone who might ask questions. Discretion is key. Some hungry recruit, someone desperate to rise. We will start with one recruit and move on if we need to."

"May I ask —"

"No, you may not. Just send me a student."

"Immediately, Lord Vader."

Without another word, the hologram faded.

How was he supposed to do this? He didn't get involved with the recruit brats. He couldn't name even one. He'd have to rely on Maggis, his second-in-command, to choose.

Sauro smiled. This was still good news. At last, a favor. His career turnaround was about to begin.

He drummed his fingers on his desk. What would make this even sweeter was if he could deliver some payback at the same time. Wasn't Bog Divinian's son enrolled in the school? It was clear to Sauro that whatever this project was, it was not something you'd want your child involved in. That would be tasty revenge.

Vader had told him the recruit should have a low profile. He couldn't ignore the direct order.

But if Bog *volunteered* his son . . . that would be different.

He just couldn't know he was being steered to do so.

Given Bog's level of intelligence, this wouldn't be a problem. The key to getting Bog to do something, Sauro had found, was to make him think he was being excluded.

He turned to his comlink. It was time Maggis called Bog in for a parent–advisor conference.

A short time later, Bog Divinian settled into the chair opposite Maggis at his desk. "So, how is my boy doing?"

"Well enough," Maggis said. "There's always an adjustment period. And since you told me that his mother was not in agreement about his training, I assume that he'll take a little time to settle in."

"I wouldn't assume that," Bog said, rankled by the suggestion. "He's a good boy. Smart boy. Takes directions well — at least when his mother isn't around. Talk about a bad influence!" He laughed, but Maggis didn't join in.

Bog didn't know how Maggis had landed this job. Only Sauro was above him. Maggis seemed lazy and out of shape, two traits Bog didn't imagine would be tolerated by the Imperial code. Maybe Sauro liked to put incompetents in positions underneath him to make himself look better.

It was only the beginning of the Empire. Lots of jockeying for power going on. The cream would rise to the top. Just as he did.

A light lit up on Maggis's console. "Excuse me, I have to take this," Maggis said.

Annoyed, Bog didn't move. The nerve of the guy, taking a comm when Bog was there! Probably some whiny parent keeping tabs on his son or daughter.

"It's from Senator Sauro," Maggis said pointedly.

"Hey, Sano is a buddy of mine. I'm sure he wouldn't mind if I listened in."

Before Maggis could move, Bog reached over and switched the comm to holo-mode. Maggis couldn't do anything — Bog was an Imperial governor.

Sano appeared in holo-form. Bog stood in front of the monitor. "Hey, surprise, old friend, it's me. Good to see you. Been meaning to contact you — I just got into Imperial City today." Not really — he'd been there a week.

"Where's Maggis?" Sauro asked.

Maggis moved forward. "Here, sir."

Sauro hesitated. Bog knew Sauro didn't want him to remain, but he couldn't ask him to leave. Bog was now several notches above him in rank, and his security clearance was now higher. Bog smiled, enjoying his former mentor's discomfort.

"Go ahead, Sano-mano," Bog said. "Maybe I can help."

"Maggis, I need a recruit volunteer for a special project," Sauro said. "He or she should be both intelligent and also have unquestioning loyalty to the Empire. Therefore, no new recruits. This comes straight from Lord Vader's office, so give it top priority."

"What's the nature of the project, sir?"

"That's on a need-to-know basis," Sauro snapped. "I want a name tonight."

"But I'd have to get parental permission —"

"There's no time. Just follow my instructions."

The hologram faded.

"Sounds like you got your tail whipped there, young fellow," Bog said.

Maggis ignored the comment. He sat down heavily.

Unlike Maggis, Bog felt exhilarated. Vader! What luck! Bog couldn't imagine how many political points he'd score by getting Lune into the program.

"I'm going to help you out here, Maggis," he said. "I'm going to volunteer my boy. You couldn't ask for a better kid. Smart. Follows orders. Loyal."

"He's very young. And he's only just arrived. Senator Sauro specified older recruits."

"Not really. You've got to learn to listen carefully. He said 'unquestioning loyalty to the Empire.' Now, that's a different thing. That's what my boy has."

Maggis stared at him. "I don't know if I'd . . . characterize your son that way."

"I would. Special boy." Bog leaned back. "I think you'd want to succeed with this one. Pleasing Lord Vader — shouldn't take that lightly. I'd be talking to Sauro, too. Telling him how helpful you were. I'm sure you want to succeed in the job. We all want to see you succeed. You have such a bright future ahead of you."

Maggis moved a durasheet from one corner of his desk to another. Bog wasn't concerned with his reluctance. He would cave. Loyalty. That's what the Empire was all about. Those who practiced it would receive their rewards. Maggis knew that.

Maggis cleared his throat. "Governor Divinian, I'll recommend your son for the project. Of course."

CHAPTER THIRTEEN

As he flew in low over the plains and cities of Acherin, Clive was shocked at the devastation. The planet had been blasted back to pre-tech times. The infrastructure had been blown to bits. The citizens were living in rubble.

When the Clone Wars began, Acherin had escaped any brushes with the conflict. They'd sided with the Separatists and were protected by an orbiting team of battleships from the Trade Federation. Their industries were too precious to lose. But a growing movement on Acherin began to side with the Republic, and after the wars ended, opposition to the Empire was fierce and vocal. Then the Imperial troops arrived, establishing garrisons and taking over major industries. Even the supporters of the Separatists joined the revolt.

The Acherins fought fiercely but were defeated. It was while under Imperial control that a civil war broke out between longstanding rival factions. The factions were concentrated in two cities, the ancient city of Eluthan and the larger, more cosmopolitan business center of Sood. The Imperials had closed their garrisons and moved all the factories off-planet. Acherin was no longer of any use to them. They left the planet without law, without government, without a power grid.

And now the devastation they left behind was being ground into dust by the Acherins themselves.

When Clive had been on the asteroid base, he'd spent time talking to its keepers, Toma and Raina, natives of Acherin. He knew about their lives before the Empire had invaded. He knew what Acherin had been. Now he saw how beings could be truly beaten and broken. They would have to rebuild their civilization from scratch without the resources to do it. But even so, the two factions were fighting each other for control, and as a result no progress could be made.

On his flight he had managed to reach Toma. Communication with the asteroid was difficult and he'd had to try again and again. When he'd reached Toma, they limited their conversation, not wanting a signal to be picked up. But Toma had managed to give him the lead he needed.

Toma had known Flame in the underground, so he'd known only her code name. She'd surfaced after the Empire had arrived. Toma had been the commander of the military arm of the resistance, so he hadn't had much direct contact with Flame. But a trusted friend had reached him on a secret comm account he had set up and told him that a former comrade needed his help.

The blockade of the planet had ended, and it was easy for Clive to land in the outskirts of the ancient city of Eluthan. There was no checkpoint, no controls. He simply hid his transport in the canyons and walked toward the walled city.

He followed the twisting streets, occasionally consulting his datapad for directions. Without landmarks, it was easy to get lost. The city bore little resemblance to the glorious place he'd heard about. The dwellings had been built of a stone that must have been beautiful once, a soft golden color that turned into liquid fire in the setting sun. But the houses and public buildings had been blasted down to stumps and repaired with plastoid parts. There were large open squares that had once held grass but now were hard-packed dirt. He could see open fires and makeshift dwellings, the shadows of Acherins preparing the evening meal. A sense of defeat rose from the stones and the ground. Clive knew that seeing this would break Toma and Raina's hearts.

He found the street he was looking for and looked for the coordinates. Any markings had long been lost. He saw a slender figure sitting on a half-blasted stairway and stopped. It was an Acherin woman, her hair short and thick with dust. Dirt streaked her tunic and one boot had a long slash down the side. It was held together with twine.

"Good evening," Clive said.

"Ah, an optimist."

He tried again. "I'm looking for Vira." Clive knew the Acherin tradition was to use first names. It was considered insulting to use someone's full name, even for a stranger. He hoped the Acherin traditions of hospitality still held.

"And who's asking?"

"Clive," he said. "Toma sent me."

This got her attention. "Toma," she breathed. "So he *is* alive."

"Alive and well and sending his regards to Vira."

"I'm sorry," the woman said. "There's no way to say this easily. Vira was killed in the fighting. She lived with us. I was her sister-in-law."

So he had come to a dead end.

She saw the disappointment on his face. "But perhaps my husband, Alder, can help you. He was good friends with Toma, too."

She stood, and he saw how tall she was. "I'm his wife, Halle. Come inside. Please."

She pushed through a makeshift plastoid door. Inside was a bombed-out building that had once been a house. A tarp served as a roof. Rubble had been cleared out and planks set on the ground for a floor. Clive noted it was swept clean.

"We don't have much, but we will gladly share," Halle said.

"Why don't you leave?" Clive asked. "There's no restriction on emigration, is there?"

"No," she answered quietly. "But this is my home. If we didn't rebuild, who would? The Empire? What kind of homeworld would we have then?"

A tattered cloth between two columns parted, and an equally tall and imposing man walked in. "Alder, this is Clive," Halle said. "Toma sent him to Vira."

Alder walked forward, a shadow in his dark eyes at the mention of his sister. "Toma? Where is he?"

"I can't tell you that," Clive replied. "But I can tell you he's well."

"Thank the moons and stars. Loss is part of our lives here now — may Vira rest with the ancients — so it's good to hear that Toma is well. Here, sit down," Alder said. "It's almost time for the evening meal."

By the looks of things, they didn't have much in the way of food. Luckily, Clive had laid in supplies. He put his utility pack on the table. "Let the visitor supply the meal. It's a custom of my world." Not really true, but he had a feeling they wouldn't accept otherwise.

"You honor us with your gift," Halle said.

Clive took out bread and protein loaf, a cylinder of prepared tea, and fruit. He added a bag of sweets and some reconstituted muffins.

Alder's eyes widened. "It's a feast!"

"First, eat. Then we can talk." Clive waved his hand at the food.

He took a few bites but mostly watched them eat hungrily. It amazed him how connected beings were to their homeworlds. He had left his homeworld of Belazura behind long ago and rarely returned. Belazura was renowned for its beauty, but Clive didn't have a particle of sentiment in his bones. He felt more comfortable moving from planet to planet. He rarely stayed anywhere long. If he had to live like this, he would have left long ago.

When he was sure they had eaten their fill, Clive poured them each a last cup of tea and sat back. "Toma told me that Vira could tell me about Flame. Flame contacted her and asked for a way to find Toma."

"Vira didn't tell us," Alder said. "She must have kept Flame's secret well."

"We knew Flame," Halle said. "Well, not before she joined the resistance — she didn't live in the old city. She was from the capital, Sood. She said she came from a wealthy family, but we didn't share much information about our personal lives."

"Do you have any idea of her real identity?" Clive asked.

Halle and Alder both shook their heads.

"You could tell she came from wealth," Alder said. "But she never put on airs, she never asked for favors. She wasn't a principal player, but she did surveillance, set up safe houses, things like that. She took the same risks we all did."

"She was very smart, very good," Halle said. "Rumors were that she smuggled much of her wealth off-planet. At first she was resented for this. Eluthans thought it showed a lack of loyalty to the homeworld. But Flame just laughed at that. She felt she would only be able to fight if she had the wealth to do it."

"She was caught by the Empire and imprisoned at the garrison," Alder said. "She managed to escape. In that escape she also rescued five members of the underground. One of them was killed, but she got the others out."

"One of them was Vira," Alder added.

Clive felt a bit sheepish. Flame truly was a hero. He had wasted his time. Time he should have been spending on Coruscant, helping Astri to rescue Lune. Everything had checked out.

So why didn't he feel better?

"Flame told Toma that her family owned some of the biggest factories on Acherin," Clive said. "And her funds do seem enormous. There can't have been that many family-owned industries. Is there a database I can check?"

Alder shook his head. "All of our records have been destroyed."

"I always thought . . ." Halle's voice faltered. "No, never mind."

"What?" Clive urged.

"Well, Flame was a good pilot. If we had a job that required flying, we gave it to her."

Clive nodded. He knew this about Flame, too.

"And once she'd mentioned to me that her father had died right before she came to us. Her grief was fresh." Halle hesitated again. "Yarrow Industries was a big manufacturer of luxury airspeeders and cruisers. Evin Yarrow died of natural causes shortly after the Empire took over his business. I know he had an adult daughter. Eve. I would imagine that a daughter raised in that industry would be an exceptional pilot."

"Yarrow Industries," Clive said. Once again he felt a distant chime inside him. Whatever memory he was chasing was elusive. Why couldn't he remember? "It sounds familiar."

"Most of their sales were confined to this system, but they were trying to break into galactic sales," Halle said. "Like most of the corporations, they sided with the Separatists. They wanted the support of the Trade Federation and the Commerce and Banking clans. I remember that Evin Yarrow kept an apartment in Galactic City on Coruscant so he could lobby the Senate."

"Was he married?"

She shook her head. "His wife died when the girl was young. I read an article about him in a holo-zine years ago. . . . I remember being impressed with how he said he raised his daughter himself, took her with him everywhere — factories, trade shows, the Senate. . . . She was a young girl then. I think there was a holo-image, but I don't remember it clearly."

"Wouldn't someone have recognized Eve Yarrow?" Clive asked.

"Not really," Alder said. "Eluthans didn't travel much to Sood."

"I don't know anything else about Eve. Our holo-news industry and all the information infrastructure collapsed around the time Flame joined us," Halle said. "We didn't ask anybody too many questions at that time. I know that the Empire eventually moved Yarrow Industries off-planet." She shrugged. "I'm probably wrong about Eve."

"Is there a reason you're asking these questions?" Alder asked.

"I need to find out if Flame is trustworthy," Clive said. "Lives depend on it."

"I would trust her with our lives," Alder said. "We *did* trust her with our lives."

Clive nodded. Made sense. But his itch was still there.

What about Halle's quiet resolve to stay and rebuild her homeworld? What about the other citizens, sticking it out, trying to rebuild with bits of plastoid and tarps?

Why had Flame left? Why had this one woman decided that she would be able, single-handedly, to create a galaxy-wide resistance movement?

Could she be Eve Yarrow? If that was true, she would have traveled the galaxy with her father. He'd had an apartment on Coruscant. What had she said again? *Never been there.* She didn't like crowded planets. She said.

Of course, he knew better than anyone that resistance fighters never told the truth about where they'd been and what they'd done.

She'd called it Imperial City, though. That bothered him. Of course Palpatine had renamed it. But every member of the resistance still called it by what they considered its rightful name, Galactic City. At least when they spoke to one another.

Well, that wasn't much to go on.

"Those people she rescued from the garrison," he said. "Can I talk to them?"

"There is only one left," Alder said. "The rest have been killed since that time, or arrested. His name is Warlin. I can contact him for you. I'm sure he'll agree to a meeting. If he's here."

"He goes to Sood undercover fairly often," Halle explained. "His daughter is married to a Sood, so he travels to see her. It's very dangerous, but . . . she's his only family."

Alder took out his comlink and entered the data. He spoke into it, quickly explaining who Clive was and asking if Warlin would speak to him.

Clive took the comlink. There was no picture, but

Warlin's voice came through clearly. "Come at dawn tomorrow," he said.

"I'd like to come tonight."

"Not possible, I'm traveling. I'll meet you at my house — Alder can lead you there." There was a burst of static, and Clive missed his next words.

"I didn't hear you — what was that?"

"I have been waiting for this. Something about . . . that day . . . always bothered me."

The communication ended. Frustrated, Clive handed the comlink back to Alder.

He would have to wait until tomorrow.

He knew he would barely sleep that night, and he didn't. It was still black outside when he rose and quietly pulled on his boots. Alder came a moment later, just a shadow in the darkness.

Without a word, Clive rose and followed him through the empty streets. The moons hung low in the sky and only the softest smudge of gray signaled the beginning of the day. Even with the bit of light it was still hard going on the pockmarked stone walkway. Occasionally they stepped into the road and slogged through the mud created by an overnight rain. The drops had snaked rivulets through the dust-shrouded plastoid. Soon, Clive was completely lost in a world of dirt and rain.

"He's just up ahead," Alder said. "And the sun is coming up."

Pale fiery light lit the edge of the building. It had come through better than most, with a whole stone wall intact. Alder walked forward and knocked on the wooden door. Clive heard the echo inside.

When no one came to the door, Alder turned to him. "Maybe he was delayed."

"Maybe." Clive stepped forward and pushed against the door. Something was against it on the other side. Something soft. With dread in his throat now, he pushed harder.

Legs. Arms. And then, with the door half-open, he saw the man, curled up, one arm outflung, sightless eyes open.

"Warlin?" Clive asked.

Alder nodded. He knelt and closed Warlin's eyes. "Rest with the ancients, my good friend," he said softly. He looked up at Clive, anguish on his face.

"This is what has happened to us," he said. "Acherins killing Acherins. Some in Eluthan thought he was a spy. He took too many chances. Just so he could see his daughter. They killed him for that."

But was that why he'd been killed? Clive wondered.

He wanted to howl his frustration. He'd never know.

CHAPTER FOURTEEN

Trever waited after lights-down. All the first-year recruits had chambers near each other. The rooms were packed tightly in a grid in the center of the complex. Every ten rooms shared a common room with banks of consoles for research purposes. From his chamber he could see the common room door.

Soon he saw Lune move like a shadow through the hallway. He slipped into the common room and the door slid shut. Technically, the recruits were supposed to retire when the lights went down, but this rule, Trever saw, was one of the few that wasn't enforced. The workload was so crushing that patrols looked the other way if students were still at dataports late at night.

Trever waited a few minutes and then darted across the hall and accessed the common room door. Lune sat at a console.

Trever sat next to him. "We should explore the

delivery points for food and materials . . . maybe there's a way out that way."

"All pickups are scanned," Lune said. "In the first week, somebody tried to get out and he was packed off to solitary for two weeks. Then he had to have a shadow, like I do."

"Okay then, do you have any ideas?"

"The hangar," Lune said. "Tomorrow we have a special piloting class there, right?"

"And?"

Lune shrugged. "We steal a ship."

"Steal a ship? Hey, that's a full moon idea. No problem. While Maggis is teaching, we just hop in the cockpit and . . ."

"No, not while he's teaching," Lune said. He turned and looked at Trever. Trever felt a jolt. Lune was younger than he was, just a skinny kid, but his intensity was spooky. He had a feeling Lune *could* figure out how to break in and steal a ship.

"You always brag about cracking security systems," Lune said.

"Well, sure," Trever said. "I can steal a transport. No problem. Maybe break into a warehouse. But this is *Imperial* security."

"Every system has a flaw. You just have to find it. I heard that somewhere," Lune said.

Trever grinned. Lune had heard it from him. He'd

heard it from Ferus. "Well, I do happen to have a couple of half-alpha charges. Not enough to blast down a hangar door, I don't think, but we could try."

Lune shook his head. "That's a last resort. If you can't hotwire the ship, we have to be able to go back to our quarters. Then we wait for another chance."

"So how are we getting into the hangar?"

"The security codes for the classrooms and hangar are changed every twelve hours. Maggis will have the code for the hangar on his security card since he's going to teach a class there first thing in the morning."

"The security card is clipped to his tunic," Trever said. "That's the first problem. The second one is that he'd notice it was gone in about two seconds flat. He needs that card to go just about anywhere."

Lune held up the card. "He doesn't need it while he's in the refresher."

"You've got to be kidding me. You stole Maggis's security card?"

"Every night Maggis takes a shower and then a long steam. He's in there for forty-five minutes, minimum. Plenty of time."

Trever shook his head at Lune's audacity. "What are we waiting for?"

The hallways were dark, but they were able to move quickly. Those reprogrammed battle droids made random checks, but they announced their imminent arrival with the clack of circuits, and they were easy to avoid, thanks to Lune's Force-ability to hear things from corridors away. They reached the hangar without being spotted.

Lune quickly swiped the card. The door slid open.

"Full moon amazing," Trever breathed. "It worked."

They hurried inside. The ships looked ghostly in the dim light, like giant creatures ready to pounce. Trever quickly headed toward the first starship, a tidy little number that was built for inner atmosphere traffic. The ramp had been left down and he raced up it and swung into the cockpit. He didn't dare start the engines yet, but he quickly flipped through a systems check.

"I'm going to have to override a security code," he whispered to Lune. "It might take a few minutes."

"Hurry."

Trever ran through the coding, trying to break it. It was more complicated than a standard security code. He tried all his tricks, but nothing worked. He went back and studied the console carefully. He'd have to think his way through this one.

"Trev, duck!"

He hesitated for only a moment and went down just as the door opened and the lights went on to full power. Footsteps started across the duracrete floor.

Underneath the console, Trever and Lune stared at each other, wide-eyed. Their only hope was to remain quiet. They had to hope that whoever it was wasn't searching for them.

The footsteps came closer. And closer. Trever felt the craft quiver as footsteps thudded up the ramp. Then boots appeared, striding into the cockpit.

A pair of dark, sleepy eyes in a pudgy face appeared, ducking under the console. "Imagine my surprise when I emerged from my relaxing steam to find my security card gone. Imagine when I plugged into security and found I was actually in the hangar."

"We were just —"

"Spare me the 'we-were-justs.' Believe me, I've heard just about every 'we-were-just' ever invented. Now squirm out, worms."

Maggis backed up so that Trever and Lune could wriggle out.

"Divinian, you stay with me. Fortin, get yourself back to your chamber. And try not to break another rule. Or run into Kestrel."

"It was my idea," Trever blurted. "Divinian shouldn't be punished, he —"

"I'm not hearing this," Maggis said. "Any more degrades and you get sent to the solitary chamber."

Trever shut up. He couldn't help Lune in solitary.

Stormtroopers marched in. "Escort Recruit Fortin to his chamber and lock him in," Maggis said. "If he moves, stun him."

The troopers surrounded Trever. He had no choice. Feeling helpless, he threw Lune one last look and walked out.

CHAPTER FIFTEEN

"C'mon," Maggis said to Lune. "This way."

Lune felt tremors of nervousness moving through Maggis. Shouldn't *he* be the one to be nervous?

He didn't know whether it was a connection to the Living Force or not, but he'd always been aware of emotions. It was one reason he'd always been afraid of his father. He'd always known how much Bog had pretended. Pretended to be a husband. Pretended to be a father. Bog's real self had leaked out no matter how much he tried to pretend.

Was it so wrong, Lune wondered for the thousandth time, not to love your own father?

It was a question he just couldn't ask his mother. He knew she would give him a careful answer. He was too young to be told the truth. Instead, Mom would call Bog "confused" or "too ambitious."

No, Mom. Dad is a bad guy.

Why was Maggis nervous? Why did he keep looking back at Lune?

He's doing something he knows isn't right.

"Where am I going?" Lune asked. For the first time, he was afraid.

"Shut up." Maggis didn't say this in a mean tone. It was more like Lune was reminding him of his own unease.

The retractable roof opened, and an airspeeder zoomed in, a sleek black number with red chromium trim. The closed cockpit rolled back and a man got out.

It was his father.

Lune stopped walking.

"No," he said.

"Your father needs you, Divinian," Maggis said. "And," he added, "I need you to follow orders. Remember, I've got your friend here. You wouldn't want anything to happen to Fortin, would you?"

Lune's mouth set. Trever could take care of himself.

Probably.

"And if you don't go, do you know who your dad will be most angry at?"

"You."

"Try again. Your mom. He blames everything on her, right? I got that much after ten minutes with him. He'll blame this on her, too."

Lune looked at Maggis. He felt the truth of what he said. It made him feel trapped.

"Son." Nervous at the delay, Bog walked forward. He smiled. It was his fatherly smile that was so fake. All Lune saw in that smile was a big empty hole.

"Don't worry, I have good news," Bog continued. "Take a ride with me and I'll tell you about it."

Dread settled inside Lune. He knew he was trapped. There was nowhere to go. He walked forward and climbed into Bog's airspeeder.

"Let me know how —" Maggis started to say to Bog, but Bog ignored him.

He settled behind the controls. The cockpit canopy slid closed and sealed Lune in.

"Hang on," Bog said with a satisfied air. "I bought this baby after I became Imperial governor. It moves."

The craft shot out into the black night. Lune didn't know Coruscant well, so he wasn't sure where they were going. He just saw a blur of skylanes and millions of lights, each of them a life going on quietly around him. He could feel them. He envied them. They were living their lives, but they weren't at the mercy of someone else. Or at least, that was what he hoped.

In his training, Garen had spoken to him about the Living Force, how some Jedi were more connected with it than others. He had talked about the great Jedi Knight, Qui-Gon Jinn. He had said that he felt a similar thing with Lune, that he could connect to the Living Force. If times were different, if he'd been identified earlier, if the Clone Wars hadn't come along . . . he could have been at the Temple, too.

The Temple was now rising in front of him, a ruin of its former self. Lune could feel the dark side of the Force in its presence, feel all the lives that had been snuffed out.

Bog chortled as he zoomed around the Temple. The Senate complex was below them now, and Bog guided the craft to a tower that rose in a far quadrant. Was his father taking him to the Senate? Lune couldn't figure it out.

Bog parked the vehicle on a landing stage, a long narrow platform that extended out like a horizontal spire.

"Don't look so nervous," he said. "This is your moment, Lunie."

Lunie. He'd always hated that nickname. He had told his father that. Many times.

Bog leaned in closer. His eyes were intense. "You get this? This is your big chance. I arranged it. Why do I bother, you ask. Because I'm your dad. Simple as that."

Bog exited the airspeeder and waited for Lune to get out. Lune followed him past a set of double doors. They entered a white hallway. He smelled medicine and cleaner. He knew this smell. He was in a hospital.

"This is where the Emperor's friends come for treatment. It's an honor to be chosen for this," Bog said. "Understand?"

Lune shook his head. He understood nothing.

Except that he was in big trouble.

Amazing that Bog Divinian's kid could have a Force connection. It must have come from Astri Oddo, not Bog. The man seemed to wear stupidity like a hat. Darth Vader watched as Bog hustled importantly into one of the EmPal conference rooms. He'd left Lune with the med droids in the adjoining examination room. They were in the main complex here and would take care of the initial steps. Then Lune would be taken to the secret rooms at the top of the tower. And Bog would go away.

Sano Sauro had told him that Bog had volunteered his own child for this assignment. Vader didn't care who Zan Arbor used for her subject, so he'd allow it. No doubt Bog would think that he would gain points for Lune's participation. Instead, he'd just added to Vader's contempt.

Bog eagerly came forward. "When I told my son the Empire needed him, he stepped up," he said. "Didn't hesitate a moment. But now that we're here, I'd like to know what exactly it is that he's volunteering *for*."

Jenna Zan Arbor looked at Vader. "Did he sign a release?"

"Not yet."

She looked exasperated. "Can I proceed without it? I don't have time for difficult parents."

"Now, who are you calling difficult? I'm easy." Bog smiled. "But I guess I have to point out, because maybe you don't know, but I'm an Imperial governor. Just want to make that clear. I've got clearance. Maybe more than you."

Zan Arbor sized him up. "I doubt it."

"So, what's the project? I deserve to be in the old laser-loop."

Vader controlled his irritation. Divinian was making a *demand*? His self-importance needed to be checked, but not here. Not yet.

He needed the boy.

"This is Dr. Zan Arbor," Vader said. "She is doing a series of tests on memory."

"That's all?" Bog looked relieved for a moment. Then his forehead creased. "But what . . . exactly will you do?"

"Pinpoint certain areas of the brain," Zan Arbor answered. "Identify memory receptors and target them for elimination."

Bog swallowed. "Elimination? What does that mean, exactly?"

"Well, obviously, some memories that the child has will disappear," Zan Arbor said. "As if they had never existed." She waved a hand. "Just inconsequential ones. Naturally I'll just take random memories from different time frames. He'll never know what's missing."

"Wait a second here," Bog said. "I don't know about this. I didn't know . . . his *brain* would be involved. Brains are important."

Zan Arbor rolled her eyes, but Vader silenced her with a look. Bog was an idiot, but he could make trouble.

Vader turned to Bog. "We all have memories we might wish to obliterate. Even a child. *Especially* a child. You could give direction to Dr. Zan Arbor."

Zan Arbor understood his meaning immediately. It would take Bog longer. She looked alert, excited. "You mean target something big? With this boy? That would be . . . helpful."

"My boy is not an experiment!" Bog boomed, but Vader wasn't about to stop.

"It is to help him," he said. "Maybe your boy has memories that could be . . . painful. Memories of . . . his mother, for example?"

He watched as Bog recoiled. And then he saw the greed take over.

Greed for control. Control of his son.

Bog licked his lips. "You could . . . pinpoint that area?"

"If you give me a time frame," Zan Arbor said. Speaking in a low tone, she drew Bog away.

Vader didn't care particularly if Bog gave permission or not, although it would be easier that way. On second thought, Lune was the perfect subject. He was Force-sensitive. Vader wasn't sure if the Force would be an obstacle to the success of the experiment. He doubted it. Lune wasn't in control of the Force, for one thing. But if, in fact, the Force would interfere with the procedure, he would need to know that.

He watched as Bog allowed Zan Arbor to take his retinal print to authorize the procedure. Then the scientist left Bog and entered the locked examination room where Lune was waiting surrounded by med droids.

"You can go now," Vader said. "I will contact you when it is time to pick him up."

Bog looked disappointed that he couldn't wait. But he knew better than to argue.

Vader turned and headed toward the inner core of the tower. Success would mean an end to torment. It was unsettling being in the place where he had learned about Padmé . . . and after the battle with Obi-Wan.

Yet there was compensation here, Sith crystals and artifacts that would restore him. And there was hope here now. Hope for the end of Padmé at last.

CHAPTER SIXTEEN

Interesting, Ferus thought. He was definitely on to something. He'd gone through the blueprints and then, once Jako had fallen into a deep snore, he'd left the room to do a visual surveillance at the Coruscant EmPal med center, using the terrace that circled the building and then some judicious Force-leaps.

He knew one thing for sure: The windowed gallery at the top of the tower was there just for show. The top of the tower wasn't the storage area the blueprints had claimed. It only looked that way.

Ferus had used a Force-technique called "thoughtful looking." It involved shifting one's concentration back and forth from the big picture to the microscopic. The method often helped a Jedi to be able to see things that even electrobinoculars didn't pick up. Ferus had seen the tiniest flaw on the metallic skin surface of the high levels of the tower. It had probably been hit by some stray debris — just a slight, glancing blow, but it was enough to ripple the metal sheeting.

And that's when he figured out that it wasn't just a durasteel scrim, but some sort of alloy used for blast protection. Probably duranium. It wasn't skin; it was armor.

Once he'd seen that, he continued his inspection until he'd found what he was looking for — the slightest of bumps, regularly spaced, indicating power feed lines. Enough power feed lines to supply a turbolaser.

He had to ask himself why a storage area needed blast protection as well as offensive weapons.

He had to get in there.

The facility was quiet now. Patients were in for the night with only regularly timed checks by the med droids. Malory had given him the schedule. Ferus walked through the halls and hopped on the turbolift. He waved his hand over the sensor for the topmost floor. He knew from the blueprints that this turbolift didn't go all the way to the top of the tower. None of the nearby ones did. No doubt there was one, but it would take him ages to find it. He only had less than an hour before the end of his shift; at dawn, his security card would become inactive and the place would start to come alive.

There was a small service turbolift, built for the med droids. It ran from the landing stage up to the tower. This turbolift also went to the landing stage and terminated there. At that point the two shafts had an access point, no doubt to allow worker access in the event of repairs or breakdown.

He hoisted himself up to the top of the turbolift and pushed through the access door. He stood on the top, balancing on the speeding cab. The numbers were a blur on the walls as the floors were counted off, but he would be able to see when the shaft ended. The only trouble was that he'd be going very, very fast.

He called on the Force. Time needed to slow down. Everything had to be absolutely clear. He needed perfect timing. And luck. Luck would be good.

Not luck, he told himself. He had to get out of those old patterns of thinking. Jedi didn't need luck. They had the Force.

He had to believe. Believe he could fly into the other shaft completely blind, not knowing if there would be something, somewhere, to grab onto.

There. There it was. Through the blackness and the rushing air he could see the ceiling of this shaft. And there, on his left, a small shift in the darkness that indicated the opening to the parallel shaft. Ferus gulped. It looked awfully . . . small. He had to have perfect accuracy in timing and position or he'd hit a permacrete wall at top speed and turn into Jedi-jam. . . .

Ferus told his mind to shut up and let the Force work.

No room for doubt.

He leaped.

He felt the Force move around him. He could see everything up close and clearly — the texture of the shaft wall, the exact quality of the darkness he was leaping toward. He flew into the other shaft with only centimeters to spare.

Immediately he saw the service turbolift several stories above. He wouldn't be able to use it to grab onto. It was stopped. It didn't surprise him; he doubted there would be med droids moving between the floors at this quiet hour. But on the other wall of the shaft he saw a power line cable bolted into the wall. Bolts big enough for handholds.

He felt the surge of the Force guiding him, and it was an infinitely easy matter to fly across the space, grab the bolts, and plaster himself against the wall. Ferus let out a breath. He'd made it. Sort of.

He made his way up the shaft using the Force and his liquid cable line. He calculated the floor he needed and found the door. It would be a squeeze, but he could make it.

He was able to activate the turbolift sensor on the outside to open the door. That was lucky. He didn't want to use his lightsaber if he didn't have to. He didn't want to leave any evidence of a Jedi break-in. He needed to be able to return to his life as a double agent.

Ferus stepped inside into a darkened room. He could feel the dark side of the Force suddenly surge. He had landed in a med droid recharging station. A line of tripedal med droids were lined up in inactive mode. Ferus walked past them toward an archway. Beyond it was a corridor that led toward the interior of the round tower.

Immediately his senses were on alert. There was activity here. Something was happening. Ferus let the noises drop away one by one. The hum of the air units and machinery, the slight buzz of the light tubes over-head. Somewhere he heard the clack of a droid making rounds, but it was several corridors away.

The Living Force was here, too.

Voices.

He crept forward. A door ahead had a small surveil-lance window. He risked a peek.

A blond human female in a luxurious cloak stood blocking his gaze into the room. Jenna Zan Arbor. What was she up to? He wasn't surprised to see her. He knew she was working for the Empire now. He'd seen her name copied on secret documents for a large-scale weapons delivery system. During the Republic, she had been a most-wanted criminal. She had introduced terri-ble viruses into populations and then offered her own vaccines to cure them. She'd made a fortune. During Ferus's very last mission, he had seen her trying to con-tact a Sith Lord on Korriban, the seat of Sith power. No, he wasn't surprised she was enmeshed with the Empire. It attracted beings like her.

He sidled around, trying to see who she was talking to. Someone was sitting on an examining table while she entered data on her medboard.

He was here to investigate Darth Vader, not track down Zan Arbor's next evil experiment. He should keep going. The chrono was ticking off the minutes. He had no way of knowing if this place would come alive with morning. And until then, anything could happen — Jako could wake up, a request for med info could come in, a random patrol could snag him. He needed to keep going. He couldn't save every being. He had to choose his battles.

Ferus turned away from the door, sensing only the presence of the dark side of the Force.

CHAPTER SEVENTEEN

Trever kicked his pillow across the room. He knew it was childish and didn't help anything. But it felt good.

He was locked in.

He had failed.

He had no doubt that from now on he would be separated from Lune. They wouldn't leave them alone together again. And they'd make sure security was tighter than before. Maybe they'd be sent to the Mining Corps. Or, even worse, they'd be here so long that they'd turn into little Imperials and march out of here in those little caps and forget their hearts and brains.

He kicked the pillow again. This was some new moon night. He didn't know how he'd ever face Astri and the others.

Soon Maggis would come for him. He'd be done with Lune. Then it would be Trever's turn.

Trever couldn't sit around and wait. He had to get out

of here. Tonight. He had to find Lune. If he waited, they would never escape.

He had his last resort hidden in his utility belt. Several sweet alpha half-charges. Not enough to blast open a hangar door, but it would do for the small door to his quarters. It would blow his cover as well as his door, but he couldn't worry about that now.

He carefully set one charge on the door. He placed his pillow over it and then one of the extra pillows he had never given back, but hidden under his sleep couch. They would muffle the sound somewhat.

He picked up the cushions from his sleep couch and used them as a wall to protect him. In these small quarters the blowback could be tricky.

The charge went off. Trever felt the explosion and was catapulted back against the wall. He peeked over the cushion. The door had been blown off its hinges. All he had to do was give it a little push in order to get out.

Leaping over the blackened fabric of the pillows and the multitude of feathers, he slammed through the door. It fell with a thud, and he ran.

He'd try the hangar first. He didn't know where else to go. Maybe Maggis would still be there with Lune.

He made his way there, racing through the dark halls, ducking into empty rooms when he heard the *click-clack* of stormtrooper boots. If they weren't in the hangar he'd search the entire place for Lune.

To Trever's surprise, the hangar door was still open.

Maggis sat slumped in a chair, his eyes closed, his head resting against the wall.

Trever stopped in the doorway, unsure of what to do. What had Maggis done with Lune?

Maggis opened his eyes, saw him, then closed them again. "Do you know what I was before this?"

Surprised at the question, Trever's answer was close to a squeak. "No."

"A professor of navigation and sublight technology. At the Celestial School of Spaceflight Engineering on Argus. Ever heard of it? Well, it's gone now. They closed it. And offered me this job. I thought, sure. How bad could it be?"

Maggis opened his eyes and looked at Trever. He looked puffy and defeated. "I'm just not in the Empire swing of things, I guess. It takes its toll."

"Oh."

"Do you know what they do to you if you quit? Happened to someone here. You're told you'll never teach again. You're blacklisted from every academy in the galaxy. Et cetera. It's the thing they do when you cross them. They lean on you until there's no breath left in your lungs. Until you have no bone or muscle left. You turn into a dry leaf. And then they just want you to . . ." he puffed out his lips and blew. "Disappear. You might as well be dead." Maggis looked around the hangar. "I liked teaching once. Oh, well."

"I'm sorry."

Trever's words seemed to wrench Maggis's attention back to him.

"Why are you here? Trying to escape again? This place more than you bargained for?"

Trever was bewildered. He didn't know whether Maggis would suddenly turn on him. "Where's Lune?"

Maggis gave him a shrewd glance. "Why do you care? You just met him today."

Trever shrugged. "I got him in trouble."

"If you say so. Well, his daddy came for him."

"Bog?"

Maggis lifted a shaggy eyebrow. "How do you know who his father is?"

"He told me."

"If you say so. Well, his daddy is an Imperial governor, so he can do what he wants. He got Lune on some special volunteer list. Big Imperial project."

"What kind of project?"

"My, my, aren't we inquisitive? Wish I could see some of this intellectual curiosity in the classroom." Maggis shook his head. "It's on a need-to-know basis, and I'm just not one of the know-it-alls. All appearances to the contrary." He gave a laugh that had only sadness in it. "Hey, but let's talk about you. What did you really hope to accomplish? Did you really think you could steal a ship?"

Trever hesitated. This was a different Maggis. Trever didn't know anything about the Living Force, but he

118

could tell that something in Maggis had changed. Or else this could be a trick. "We were just fooling around."

"I told you already, no more 'we-were-justs.' You're not some kid with Imperial stars in your eyes, are you? I knew something about you didn't fit," Maggis said, but he said it absently, as if he were really thinking of something else.

He looked around the hangar. Then he put his hands on his knees and took a breath.

"Okay," he said. "Let's go."

"Where?" Trever asked. He was prepared to run. He could outrun Maggis, unless Maggis had a stun blaster. Which he probably did.

"Anywhere but here, kid. I'm your ticket out, Fortin. Or whatever your name is." Maggis crooked a finger at a transport. "That one?"

Was it a trick?

"Hurry up before I change my mind. You caught me on a good night. I'm sick of the Empire, and I'm sick of this hat." Maggis tossed his officer's cap across the hangar.

He had to take the chance. Trever moved forward. He didn't quite believe this was happening. He started up the ramp to the cockpit.

Kestrel's voice suddenly echoed across the hangar. "What's this, an early morning class? Nobody told me."

"Recruit Kestrel, how good of you to join us." Maggis drawled the words.

Trever froze.

Maggis jerked a shoulder toward Trever. "Recruit Fortin has decided to take a joyride on an official Imperial cruiser. Unofficially."

Kestrel took several brisk steps forward. Despite the fact that it was the middle of the night, he was fully dressed in his uniform. "Allow me to do the honors, sir. I'm Fortin's shadow. I'm responsible for his behavior. I have to tell you that his door has been blown off its hinges."

"Now *that's* determination," Maggis said. "You're obviously taking your job just as seriously, Kestrel. Who knew I had such dedicated recruits on my hands?"

Kestrel's hand was on his holster. "Allow me to take care of this, sir."

"Be my guest. For this offense, I'd say twenty-five degrades should do it. That should guarantee Fortin makes it to the Mining Corps by the end of the week, at the rate he's going."

Trever braced himself, ready to jump as Kestrel reached for his blaster. But before Kestrel could get it out of his belt, Maggis moved with surprising swiftness. He drew his own blaster and aimed it at Kestrel.

"I think I should tell you that this is a real one," he said in a friendly tone. "The sting is slightly more . . . unpleasant."

Kestrel's neck flushed. "I don't believe you."

Blasterfire streaked across the hangar and blew up a service console.

Maggis backed up the ramp, still holding the blaster on Kestrel. "Get inside," he told Trever. "Start up the engines."

"What are you doing, sir?" Kestrel was incredulous.

"It appears, Recruit Kestrel, that my brilliant but short Imperial career is at an end. Enjoy."

Suddenly Kestrel streaked toward the security panel. He hit the sensor, and the alarms sounded.

Maggis could move fast when he had to. He leaped into the cockpit, jumped into the pilot seat, and grabbed the controls.

He activated the retractable canopy, but it stopped halfway, shut down by the security system. He quickly overrode the system with a code and it began to close again. "Here's where I get to prove I can actually fly," he said to Trever.

Angling the craft sideways, he cleared the canopy by millimeters as it slid shut, clipping the ship and sending it in a spiral that Maggis corrected by flying upside down. Then they shot out into the lights of the Coruscant night.

CHAPTER EIGHTEEN

Ferus passed room after room of equipment and diagnostics, but no record consoles. Sweat beaded his hairline. He felt it break out on his legs and arms and trickle down his back. Was there something in the air-filtering system that was making him dizzy? A lack of oxygen? There was something about this feeling that felt familiar.

Korriban.

He had felt like this on Korriban. When along with the Padawans and their Masters they had gone into the great valley of the Sith, into their very tombs. That radiating energy had caused them to feel dizzy and sick.

He paused. He must be near Sith artifacts. Maybe a Holocron. That would explain it.

Well, he had conquered the feeling then, as a boy of sixteen. He could do it again. He just had to keep going.

Then the voices began.

You know now where your path lies.

It lies with us.

A shift happened, as though a new sensor had clicked on inside his body. His head cleared. Suddenly everything went sharp and bright. He felt the call, and it lured him, as if a string had been tied to his breastbone and tugged. Tugging him toward the source. Power lay there. Why was he resisting it?

This is what Emperor Palpatine was trying to tell him. Exploring the dark side of the Force wasn't dangerous. It was natural.

Go to the source of the power. You will see then what you can do. More than you ever thought possible.

He moved forward. Ahead of him was an open door. Identical to all the others, brushed durasteel, but he could feel the pull. He slid up against the wall next to the opening and peered inside the chamber. It was several stories high, and this was the top, where a catwalk ran around the circular space. Along the walls, ancient weapons were stored in cases. Ferus didn't recognize them, but he did recognize their powerful aura of doom. He took a few steps forward onto the catwalk and looked down.

Below, ten stories down, he saw the top of Darth Vader's helmet. He stood in the center of the open chamber, his back to Ferus, intent on what was in his open palm. A Holocron.

A Sith Holocron. Vader held it in his gloved hands, as if gaining power from it.

Ferus felt a powerful urge. With the Holocron in the

room, would he be able to draw power from it and engage his enemy? His hatred for Vader surged and joined with the waves of the dark side of the Force. He felt it pulse through his body. He remembered how he had destroyed the room at the garrison simply by joining his anger to the Force. He could fight Vader. At this moment he felt powerful enough to bring the whole tower down with him. He could come at him from above.

He would have vengeance for Roan.

And it would be sweet.

A tiny voice ordered him to step back. He tried to ignore it. There was still a voice there, a voice of a Jedi — of Siri, of Obi-Wan, his own younger voice — that told him the dark path was the path of madness and no return and he must resist. He wanted to stamp on that voice, grind it under his boot. Instead, it grew. He couldn't hear and couldn't breathe. He stepped back and pressed himself against the wall.

His last memory of Roan rose in his mind. The memory that gave him so much pain. He thought of the look in Roan's eyes. Roan had said good-bye, but also . . . *do not let this corrupt you.*

Roan had always known him better than he knew himself.

He eased away. He still felt shaky. He had to understand that the dark side of the Force would find the arrogance that lay dormant in him and inflame it. He wasn't ready to confront Vader. He was coming close to an edge he couldn't even see.

He mustn't be deflected. He still felt instinctively that the key to defeating Vader was in discovering his true identity. Ferus hurried down the hall and turned the corner. There had to be a central console for the droids to access. The time to find it was now, before . . . before he made a mistake. There was danger here, and it wasn't from prowler droids and stormtroopers.

He found it, at last, outside the entrance to the operating suites. A medical diagnostic station. Ferus could use his EmPal access code to start, then see what kind of security walls he ran into.

He quickly found the records. They were coded, of course, but this wasn't the impenetrable code of Darth Vader. It was no doubt an encryption that had been done by an Imperial coder, installed when the system had been set up, and used by a records droid who inputted the password each time it accessed the system. Which meant if Ferus could find the string, he could break the code.

He slipped a device out of his belt and into the drive. Strictly illegal, but it had its uses.

Within seconds, he had found several likely strings of code. They were frequently entered so any one could be a password. He inputted them one after the other. By the tenth, he had the password. Lucky. He was in.

Ferus quickly searched back to the end of the Clone Wars, when the first reports of Darth Vader had surfaced. It was shortly after the Emperor seized full power.

There were constant shipment orders before that time. The Emperor had been creating this secret surgical center for months. There were no patients, however. Down in the EmPal that everyone knew about, there was a constant stream of the wealthy and powerful. But up here, there didn't seem to be any. This was such an exclusive club that there weren't any members. Had it been set up just for Palpatine's needs alone? Or were records expunged as soon as the patient was treated?

How about equipment? Ferus's fingers flew over the keys. Bacta shipments, totally normal. Full body scanners. He ran through various medical devices. He recognized some, but not others. He wasn't a medical mastermind. He'd have to commit them to memory and then run them by Amie Antin.

He thought again of Zan Arbor and the patient he'd seen. Well, he hadn't seen the patient. Zan Arbor had blocked whoever it was.

Ferus's fingers stopped moving. He thought back to the glimpse he'd had inside that room.

She'd blocked whoever it was. He couldn't see anything, just a corner of a tunic.

It had been a child. Zan Arbor couldn't have blocked

a human adult. And Malory had told him that no other species were allowed at EmPal.

A child.

Ferus looked at the screen. The information was there. All he needed was time. He could keep digging, find more information, and piece by piece, he could have a picture of what this place was and if Darth Vader had been treated here.

Yes, there was his vengeance. But now there was this child. A child he didn't know.

Roan, what should I do?

There was no answer, because Roan was dead. He would never hear his voice again.

He turned away from the console. He wrenched his attention away from the letters and numbers on the screen. He powered it down. The ghost images blinked off.

He left the room.

He was confused. What was he? Not quite a Jedi. Could he somehow progress to the full power of a Jedi Knight without the structure of the Temple and the wisdom of the Council? Could he do it on his own?

Didn't he *need* the lessons the Emperor could give?

He was strong enough to resist the pull of evil. He could still access the best part of himself.

He was still a person who would be moved by the fate of a child.

He retraced his steps to the examining room where he'd seen Zan Arbor. It hadn't been more than ten minutes since he'd seen her.

He sidled up to the door. He took the same glimpse inside.

This time he saw the child.

Lune.

Relief poured through him. To think he could have turned away! He had come so close to making the wrong choice. He would have turned his back on Astri's son.

Was this what the dark side of the Force would do to him?

Another med technician entered, a human woman. Ferus experienced a shock when he realized he'd met her before. It was Linna Naltree, the sad-eyed scientist who'd been recruited to work on Ussa. What was she doing here? Had she joined Zan Arbor in her terrible work by choice? Impossible.

She crossed to Lune and laid a hand on his shoulder. Her fingers squeezed gently in reassurance. Anger crossed her face as she looked over at Zan Arbor.

This could be his way out. Linna would help them.

If Zan Arbor didn't leave the room, he'd have to go in with his lightsaber. He'd rather avoid that. He needed as much lead time as he could get. Darth Vader was on the premises. If he thought about it too long, he'd realize he didn't stand a chance.

He was in danger from the Sith Holocron, but the

Force was still here. He had to trust it. It was here, it was everywhere, even in the midst of evil. He could pull it from the air, and it could protect him and feed him. He had to remember the feeling that had led him here, to a child he thought he didn't know. That feeling was what connected him to the Living Force.

He concentrated on Zan Arbor. He sent the Force toward her, hoping that he could affect her mind. He'd never been particularly good at it as a Padawan. He had been too rigid, Siri had told him. Too set in his own mind patterns to influence anyone else.

Well, he was no longer rigid.

Go and double-check everything. Can't make a mistake. Go over the material in solitude. In solitude.

He sent the thought toward her and waited the split second that seemed like an eternity.

She shook her head slightly, then left the room by the other door.

Ferus didn't hesitate. He burst in. Linna looked up, startled. Lune smiled.

"I knew you'd come," he said.

"I don't want to get you in trouble," Ferus said to Linna. "But I'm taking Lune out of here."

"You're taking me, too," Linna said. "I can't stay here anymore. That woman is monstrous."

It was more than he'd bargained for, but she'd smuggled Trever out from under the Imperial troops. He owed her. "All right. Hurry." They exited the room and ran down the corridor. "Where did you come in?" Ferus asked.

"A landing stage," Lune said. "Bog brought me."

"How did you get up to this level? A turbolift?" Lune nodded.

A turbolift that wasn't on the blueprints. He'd guessed there must be one. "Can you find it again?"

"I think so."

"Were there any vehicles when you came inside the complex? Airspeeders? Ambulances?"

"Bog had an airspeeder, but he left."

"I came with Zan Arbor," Linna said. "There's a small hangar off the landing stage. One standard-issue small ambulance — a medspeeder. You can load one patient in the back."

"Okay, we're going to have to try that. Lead the way, Lune."

Lune led them through the maze of dark corridors and down several ramps. He didn't hesitate once. Finally they reached the turbolift. Ferus waved his hand over the sensor, hoping it wasn't coded. He saw the indicator light flash.

"Good," he murmured.

They watched the sensor indicate that the turbolift was ascending toward them. Then suddenly the light shifted to red and began to blink. The turbolift suddenly shut down.

Ferus's heart sank. It had to be a security alert.

"They know Lune is missing," Ferus said. "We have to go my way."

Ferus's mind worked quickly as he led them down to the droid recharging station. So far it wouldn't be a full-scale alert. Lune was missing, but they wouldn't assume he'd been taken by someone from the outside . . . not yet. They might assume that Linna had taken him for another test . . . or that he had run away, and she was looking for him. They wouldn't assume the worst. They had a few minutes. But no doubt prowler droids would be sent out to look for them.

Just as he had the thought, he saw the droid. Ferus wondered if it had blast capability as he unclipped his lightsaber.

Blasterfire streaked toward them. He deflected it and sent it back. The prowler droid went down, smoking.

"We'd better hurry. There'll be more."

He led the others to the glass-walled gallery that ran around the tower. It was deserted. Outside it was still dark. Travel in the skylanes was still light in the predawn hour, just a sprinkling of colored lights moving through the illumination cast by millions of glowlights on the elevated walkways and canyons of commerce. Ferus looked down at the tower itself, trying to reconcile the blueprints he'd studied with his own impressions.

Linna looked down, too. "It's a free fall down to

the landing stage," she said. "How can we get down there?"

"Let me worry about that." He *was* worried. With his Force-ability, Lune could probably make it. But what about Linna?

Suddenly he felt a warning. Ferus reacted quickly, pulling Linna and Lune down just as blasterfire ricocheted through the gallery.

Five prowler droids winged toward him in star formation, firing rapidly as their photoreceptors detected Lune and Linna. The air was full of smoke. Ferus triple-somersaulted through the air. His lightsaber arced and danced as he swung, deflecting the fire and sending all five droids crashing to the floor.

Ferus was so attuned to the Force now that he could sense the air displacements outside in the corridor. More prowler droids were approaching. He had no doubt that Vader would be next. Thousands of meters in the air, they were trapped.

The only way was straight out, then down.

Ferus felt something strange, a humming in his bones that spread suddenly throughout his chest, like a burning star. Power. It seemed something apart from him, something he could reach out and tap if he wanted. This wasn't the fluidity of the Force, it was something different in quality. The dark side of the Force that could be grasped in a fist and used.

If he wanted.

And he heard the voices again, but this time they weren't outside of him. They were inside, at the heart of the humming inside him. Ferus turned and looked at the transparisteel. Any moment he expected to see a flock of droids approaching.

You can save them.

All you have to do . . . is this.

The transparisteel window exploded inward, showering the corridor with jagged remnants of what had been solid a moment before.

"Ferus?"

Lune wasn't practiced in the Force, but he felt enough to be afraid.

Ferus saw his reflection in the shattered glass. His eyes, glowing. His lip, curled. His face, dark with anger. He didn't recognize himself.

Not understanding, Linna touched his arm. He looked at her hand and wanted to rip it off his body. He didn't want connection.

"You can't make it with me," Linna said. "And you have to save Lune."

Stupid woman, choosing to stay when I can save you!

Whose thought was that? His?

What is happening to me?

The voices . . .

"Go," Linna urged. "They don't know I was with you yet. I can go back. Remember you have a friend here."

She turned and ran, jumping over the shards of transparisteel and disappearing.

Ferus hadn't expected that. He stared at the empty air where Linna had stood. She had wanted so badly to escape. Yet she'd gone back to them.

Sacrifice had no place in a Sith's galaxy.

Where did he want to live? With beings like Linna, or like Vader?

He felt the dark side drop away.

Ferus looked over the side, down thousands of meters to the narrow shelf of the landing stage.

He looked at Lune. "Trust your feelings. Remember?"

"Don't think," Lune said. "Just do."

"I promise you," Ferus said, "we can do this."

Ferus clipped a line from his belt to Lune's. Then, calling on the Force, he didn't think, didn't hesitate, didn't wonder. He leaped.

CHAPTER NINETEEN

The Imperial starship screamed through the night sky, zooming between buildings and underneath sky-walks. Apparently Maggis did not believe in skylanes.

As they barely cleared a high-rise, Trever cleared his throat. "Uh, do you think we should slow down?"

"I just got my freedom back, kid. Let me enjoy it." Despite his words, Maggis pulled back on the speed. "Where to?" he asked.

"I need to find Lune. And I think you know more than you're telling me."

Maggis didn't answer. He zoomed into a skytunnel.

"I can help you," Trever said. "I know people here on Coruscant. They can give you new ID docs. Concoct a fake background. You could even teach again. They know how to bury you so deep the Empire could never find you."

Maggis chewed on his lower lip. They emerged out of the skytunnel into the warehouse district. Maggis zoomed around a loading dock, then made an abrupt turn and flew under it, reversing his direction.

"I think I know where he is," Maggis said. "I won't rescue him. I'm no hero. But I'll fly you there."

They flew through the skylanes. Soon it was apparent to Trever that they were heading back to the Senate district. They circled over the Senate complex and headed toward a tall tower with an oval bulb-like crown on top of it.

"EmPal," Maggis said. "One of the Emperor's pet projects."

"A med facility? Why did Bog take Lune there?"

"Like I said, he volunteered him," Maggis said with a sneer. "His *boy.*"

Trever peered at it as they flew closer. Something caught his eye, a reflection. Something was weird. He grabbed for a pair of macrobinoculars.

"The transparisteel . . ." he muttered. "It's shattered."

"Nothing to do with me. I'll put you down near the emergency entrance."

Then Trever saw something unexpected. A boy falling out of the sky.

Maggis turned the starship, and Trever flipped over on the seat and strained to focus his macrobinoculars.

"Slow down! It's Lune! He's falling!" Another body floated into the macrobinocular scope. Trever slowly realized the man was tethered to Lune, and it was Ferus.

"We've got to help them!"

Maggis twisted to look at him. "I said I was no hero!"

Blasterfire streaked out of the tower. And then . . . Trever gulped. Was that *cannonfire?*

"Great novas — that's a laser cannon!" Maggis roared, turning the ship.

"Get down there — they're falling toward the landing stage!"

"Are you crazy?"

"They won't fire on you! You're in an Imperial ship!"

"I kinda don't want to take that chance, kid!"

Trever threw himself over at Maggis and pushed the controls. The ship dipped.

"All right, all right!" Maggis's jaw set.

Maggis flew the ship down, zigzagging all the way and flying at top speed.

Trever pressed his face against the windscreen, trying to keep Ferus in sight. His only hope was if Ferus saw them. And recognized that despite appearances, they weren't the enemy.

Time seemed leisurely to Ferus. Amazing he could feel so calm while hurtling down thousands of meters. Trust flowed between him and Lune. In the midst of the rushing stars and air, Ferus felt a strange exhilaration. He was at the center of himself now, in tune with the complex Living Force that throbbed in the millions of beating hearts in Galactic City. And he wasn't afraid.

The platform below rushed toward him. He sighted on the sensor spike he'd seen from above. He reached for his laser line. He unfurled it, watched it snake through the black night and wrap around the sensor spike. The line went taut, and he and Lune bounced wildly. The line held.

The spike had broken his fall, and now all they had to do was make an easy Force-leap of a hundred meters or so, down to the landing stage. Then a quick dash into the hangar, and . . .

The stormtroopers poured out on the landing stage. They were equipped with light missile launchers.

And they were hanging here, perfect target practice.

Ferus began to swing. His only hope now was to swing them up to the sensor spike, and somehow crawl back to the tower itself. Except there was no way into the building that he could see.

The first blast missed them by centimeters. Lune cried out.

"Swing!" Ferus ordered, and Lune began to swing his legs, trying to create the momentum to get them away from the targeting computers.

Great. Now an Imperial starship was heading toward them. Something small and fast. Probably equipped with laser cannons. Someone was already trying to do

a visual sighting. He could just make out a̶̶̶̶
the windscreen.

If he could manage to reach the alpha charge in i̶̶
utility belt . . .

"Turn on the cockpit lights!" Trever yelled.

"What for? So those troopers can aim straight at our heads?"

"Just do it! It'll be okay."

Cursing, Maggis switched on the cockpit lights. Trever pressed himself against the windscreen as Ferus did a slow turn.

Ferus smiled. He'd recognized Trever.

"Okay, you can switch them off. Now open the cockpit canopy and get underneath them."

"Are you nuts? They can't just drop in! The speed ratio is too fast. They can't judge it. They'll miss!"

"He can do it. Trust me."

Maggis brought the starship in line. "I'm just doing one pass, just one. Then I'm outta here."

He turned the ship and zigzagged his way toward Ferus and Lune. A missile streaked toward the pair, and Ferus somehow managed to get out of the way.

A second later, Maggis zoomed underneath them. With split-second timing, Ferus directed Lune to climb on his back and released the laser line.

The two fell through space, straight down. Ferus

guided them into the opening and they landed in the cockpit with a jolt that sent the starship lurching. They sprawled on the floor.

"Holy moon!" Maggis blustered. He pushed the engines forward, and they shot away, cannonfire streaking behind them.

Ferus lay half-sprawled on the floor, his arm securely around Lune. Trever stared at them, wild-eyed. He couldn't believe it had all worked.

"I don't know how you did it," Ferus said, looking around at the Imperial ship, "but thanks." He looked over at Maggis, in his Imperial officer's uniform. "And thanks to you, too, whoever you are."

"That's whoever-you-are, *sir*," Maggis corrected, wiping the sweat off his face.

CHAPTER TWENTY

Once Lune was returned to his mother in a safe house in Galactic City, she did not let him out of her sight for twenty-four hours. Then Dex gently suggested that Lune might need some time to play, and she let him go off to play laser tag with a group of kids who lived on Thugger's Alley.

Dex had sent Maggis on to another safe house, where he promised they would set him up with a new identity. Flame and Wil had arrived from Bellassa, and Clive had joined them as well. It was time to plan the first Moonstrike meeting. It would have to be done in a place of complete safety.

"Well, now, you can meet here, I suppose," Dex said. "But —"

Flame was already shaking her head. "I don't think anyone would agree. No one wants to meet right under the Emperor's nose."

Keets and Curran Caladian both started to speak at

once, coming up with different suggestions. Clive watched as Astri faded out of the room. He followed.

"Are you going to join Moonstrike?" he asked.

She shook her head. "I don't really have a home-world. I lived all over with Didi when I was a girl. Then we settled here in Galactic City. But technically I'm not part of the resistance."

"This could be a place to begin," Clive said.

"Ry-Gaul has offered to train Lune," she said. "The Jedi think he can develop his Force-ability. He'll never be a Jedi, but he could be . . . something. I owe him that. I guess I can't run from his Force-ability any longer. So we'll stay here for the time being."

"Maybe I have a job for you," Clive said. "There's something I need to do." He nodded in the direction of the conference. "We're placing a lot of trust in Flame. She's passed enough tests, it's true. But . . ."

"But what?"

"I don't trust her."

"So? You don't trust anybody."

"I went to Acherin to look into her background. I might have stumbled on her real identity. I thought I found somebody who might know something, but he was killed before I got a chance to talk to him. That bothers me."

Astri frowned. "Isn't Acherin in the middle of a civil war?"

"Yeah."

"With people getting killed every day?"

"Well, okay. Maybe it looks right. It just doesn't smell right. Flame escaped an Imperial prison with five others. All of them are either dead or back in prison. There's no way to trace what that operative might have known. And all the records on Acherin are gone. There's no way to trace who Flame really is. That bugs me."

"You realize that if you start digging, you might do more harm than good. Might stir something up that the Empire can use. And that could be the end of Moonstrike."

"Yeah, that's occurred to me." Clive hesitated. "You know, you were wrong before. It isn't true that I don't trust anybody. I trust Ferus. And you. I need help."

"Hmm, Clive Flax is asking for help. Never thought I'd see the day." Astri sighed. "All right. I guess I could use a distraction."

It wasn't exactly a rousing show of support, Clive thought, but it was a start.

Ferus was due at the Imperial landing platform. But first there was someone he needed to contact.

Obi-Wan appeared in holo-mode in only seconds. His beard was streaked with more silver, and deep lines etched his cheeks. "I haven't heard from you in awhile," he said.

"You don't look so good," Ferus said.

"Charming as ever," Obi-Wan said. "I could say the same. What's going on?"

"Roan is dead."

The spasm on Obi-Wan's face told him how deeply the news had struck him.

"How?"

"Vader."

Obi-Wan looked off. Ferus tried to imagine what he saw. The dirt and rocks of Tatooine. The dust of his exile.

"I'm sorry," Obi-Wan said.

"And a Jedi has surfaced," Ferus said. "Someone you know. Ry-Gaul."

The sorrow on Obi-Wan's face eased. "I'm glad to hear that news."

"I'm gaining more trust within the Empire," Ferus went on. "I've been given a special assignment from Palpatine. Find any Force-adepts."

"A special assignment? I don't like the sound of that. You can't underestimate Palpatine. He is vastly more powerful than you. So is Vader. Together they're . . ."

"Unbeatable?"

"For you alone, yes."

"I know that," Ferus said. "But there are still things I can do. I've met someone, a contact who is trying to organize a resistance, planet to planet —"

"It's too soon," Obi-Wan said abruptly.

"Your considered opinion," Ferus said, "as a hermit living in the Outer Rim?"

"I may be in exile, but I know the Empire," Obi-Wan said sharply. "Resistance must be built slowly. The

Empire has a lock on power right now. It's been able to move from system to system and its communication network is already in place."

"Imperials are not the only ones with power," Ferus countered. Obi-Wan was lecturing him again.

"Just keep your focus where it already is," he said. "Are there any true prospects for the Force-adepts?"

"A few," Ferus said. "I was given a list." He told Obi-Wan of the different subjects on it.

He thought Obi-Wan would focus on the bounty hunter or the teacher, just as he had, but Obi-Wan went very still.

"The baby on Alderaan."

"Didn't seem promising," Ferus said. "A railing gave way, someone didn't fall . . . sounds more like a coincidence than anything. Someone's attempt to curry favor higher up the line with the Imperials. There are informers in every city on every planet these days. Even on a planet like Alderaan. But every report gets followed up, so it made its way to me."

"You must file a report dismissing the sighting," Obi-Wan said. "But first you must go to Alderaan and seem to investigate it."

"I have more important things to do than chase down a false lead," Ferus said. "I have a couple of real leads to look into."

"No," Obi-Wan said. "This is the most important thing you must do."

Ferus wanted to tell Obi-Wan that he couldn't give him orders, but he didn't think that would stop him from issuing them.

"Is there anything else I should know?" he asked.

Obi-Wan frowned. "I'm telling you what you need to know. And that isn't everything."

"You know," Ferus said, exasperated, "this isn't the Temple, I'm not a Padawan, and you aren't the Jedi Council."

A ghost of a grin crossed Obi-Wan's face. "I know. But I'm all you've got."

And then the smile faded, and across the billions of stars separating them, they touched each other's grief. Ferus's words conjured up the silence and hush of the Temple, the humming energy of the classrooms, the ring of boots on ancient stone, the laughter of the younglings. The Council chamber, all twelve Jedi Masters sitting in a circle, with their experience, their wisdom, and their strength. They felt the loss of it, fresh and keen as the day it had all been destroyed.

When Ferus spoke again, his voice was soft and measured.

"I'll leave today," he promised.

If Obi-Wan said it was important, he would trust that it was.